My Dead and Blackened Heart

Andrew Freudenberg

Further books by the Sinister Horror Company:

THE UNHEIMLICH MANOEUVRE – *Tracy Fahey*

TRYING TO BE SO QUIET & OTHER HAUNTINGS – *James Everington*

THE CHARNEL CAVES: A CRABS NOVEL – *Guy N. Smith*

WHAT GOOD GIRLS DO – *Jonathan Butcher*

MARKED – *Stuart Park*

HELL SHIP – *Benedict J. Jones*

CORPSING – *Kayleigh Marie Edwards*

FOREST UNDERGROUND – *Lydian Faust*

CANNIBAL NUNS FROM OUTER SPACE! – *Duncan P. Bradshaw*

KING CARRION – *Rich Hawkins*
MANIAC GODS – *Rich Hawkins*

PUNCH – *J. R. Park*
UPON WAKING – *J. R. Park*
DEATH DREAMS IN A WHOREHOUSE – *J. R. Park*
MAD DOG – *J. R. Park*

GODBOMB! – *Kit Power*
BREAKING POINT – *Kit Power*

I DREAM OF MIRRORS – *Chris Kelso*

Visit SinisterHorrorCompany.com for further information on these and other coming titles.

SINISTER HORROR COMPANY

PRESENTS

MY DEAD AND BLACKENED HEART

ANDREW FREUDENBERG

My Dead and Blackened Heart

Edited by J. R. Park
Design by J. R. Park
Cover and interior illustrations by Xavier Freudenberg

Published by The Sinister Horror Company

My Dead and Blackened Heart -- 1st ed.
ISBN 978-1-912578-14-6

To Mike,

Keep publishing the great books! Hope you find something to enjoy within.

ACKNOWLEDGEMENTS

A special thank you to all of my writing friends for their encouragement, and to all of the publishers that have printed my stories.

An extra very special thanks to Justin Park, and the Sinister Horror Company, for their support and hard work.

Fred

To my wonderful Mum, Wendy, my Ninja wife Sal, and my monkey boys, Zac, Otsi, and Xavi. Thank you for all the things.

Contents

SOMETHING AKIN TO DESPAIR

Warminster woke as soon as he felt the first rays strike the solar panels. Although sleep was not a necessity, he was a fool for routine and had made a habit of it.

"Lights."

He could see perfectly well in the dark but he preferred to adhere to convention. Standing quickly, he made his way to the dining room. Once there he helped himself to a bowl of decomposing raw protein powder. The machinery designed to turn it into something edible no longer functioned, but he liked to keep up appearances, even in solitude.

"Audio library. Wagner."

As music filled the air, he pushed his meal aside. He had breakfasted alone here more than a hundred thousand times and he was weary of it. The bustle and banter of the multitude that had lived and worked here remained fresh in his memory. Never to forget; that was the curse for one such as him. Coupled with what seemed to be eternal life, it was a heavy burden.

"End audio."

He strode through the empty corridors, taking care not to step on the bones of his former associates. Once again he slowed as he passed the intertwined skeletons of two that he had dared to call friends.

"Warminster do something…"

There had been nothing he could do except watch them die. "Warminster…"

His ability to understand regret and loss had grown over the lonely years and every day this pair gave him particular pause for thought. The way that they held onto each other, even in death, never failed to trigger something akin to despair deep in his gut.

"Sorry…"

Respects paid he carried on walking. The passage widened out into a broad thoroughfare. Signposted double doors led to a variety of further rooms on either side; 'Medical Centre', 'Administration', 'Robotics' and so on. All were now staffed only by corpses, a once lively routine replaced by the literal graveyard shift.

The various systems embedded in these tombs of plastic and steel still murmured to him, ghosts in the machine, their functionality obliterated by the disaster that had befallen their masters. The monitoring of their wellbeing had once been his main purpose and it pained him to be reminded of their fate. Still, he couldn't bring himself to silence the constant drip of data, as easy as that would have been.

"Patient area contaminated… service requests ignored… local life support non-optimal…"

The entire base was redolent of bereavement, and he felt broken by the loss. The hole left by the absence of any human crew was devastating to all that remained in this dysfunctional existence.

As he passed beyond the individual departmental data-spheres their influence waned, becoming little more than background noise. The main dome containing the nuts and bolts of the mining operation loomed before him with its own litany of mechanical suffering.

"Outer wall breach in effect… drill module malfunction… unexpected contaminant detected…"

The cause of their distress was a huge hole where the

explosion had torn through both the outer and inner walls. Through this gaping wound, many times higher than him, Warminster could see the curve of this icy moon stretching away into darkness. Just beyond the dome, twisted metal girders and other remnants of the catastrophe littered the ground. The communications dish had been torn in two by the blast and its remains sat amidst this display of carnage. A sprinkling of bodies lay alongside, their anguished expressions frozen for eternity.

"Repair mode unsuccessful… warning, post unattended…"

He closed his eyes and let the chatter wash over him for a couple of minutes. Finally he opened them again and took a deep breath. It was not for the oxygen, of which there was none, but for the sensation that the cold air gave him.

Skirting around the tall oblong buildings that capped the dig he continued walking. Not for the first time he felt pain in his lower legs. He was degrading, showing signs of wear after all these years. When he looked at himself in the mirror he could see that his once glowing skin had blanched and was flaking away in places. There were dark patches on his hands and he could see metal poking through on a couple of his fingers. If life had continued uninterrupted then he could have been revitalized… if he wasn't all alone.

"Searching…"

Although it was barely a whisper, the voice boomed in Warminster's head. He knew every machine, every source of distraction, and this was something new.

"Scanning…"

It hadn't come from within the dome. Impossibly it seemed to be coming from orbit. He ran, a floodgate of emotions opening inside his head. In moments he was outside, clambering up the jagged edges of the dome.

"Performing low level sweep… assessing damage…"

He could see it now. It was a silver sphere, shining a single spotlight down over the surface of the moon. It was moving towards the base at a steady speed.

"Searching for life signs…"

Warminster clambered up onto the warped strut to which he had been clinging. As the craft passed overhead, illuminating him, he waved his arms in the air.

"I'm here! I'm here!"

For a moment it paused. Warminster watched it, eyes wide open and heart in his mouth.

"Zero organic life detected. Reconnaissance aborted."

The craft shot up into the heavens. Warminster let out a screech of torment and fell to his knees. Had he any tears he would have shed one but it was beyond him. His dream of humanity was just that; an empty fantasy that he should never have allowed himself to foster. He was a machine, a tool, and that was all he would ever be.

A BITTER PARLIAMENT

The sun was long gone by the time they finally pulled up outside the cabin. Finding it had turned into an epic task after they became hopelessly lost on the narrow country paths leading up into the hills. Eventually they had happened upon a dour faced farmer, and he had pointed them towards the forest road. Perhaps road was too fancy a word for the pitted mud trail that wound in amongst the trees, but they had expected that. The old man on the phone had been insistent that they would need four-wheel drive.

"If you come in one of those mobile crumple zones then you'll get stuck for sure. Like my advert said, the place is well off the beaten track."

Their SUV, only ever tested by the tepid challenges of rush hour in London, had performed admirably. Dan admitted some of the steeper inclines had caused him some concern but they made it. They could worry about the journey back later and just enjoy their minor victory over the English countryside.

Maria released her seatbelt and climbed out of the car. The smell of pine and dank earth filled her nostrils. She shivered as she walked round to the tailgate and opened it.

"Yes Shark. You can get out now. We're here."

The large Rottweiler inside needed no second telling and threw himself out onto the dirt. He stretched, gave the cold night air a sniff, and wandered off to answer the call of nature.

"I've found the key!"

Maria looked over to where Dan was holding up his prize between finger and thumb and smiled. He had taken no little persuading to make this trip, but he seemed determined to try and make the best of it. A nice hotel with a well stocked bar was more his speed, however she had wanted to do something different, something far from other people.

To say that she was on the verge of a nervous breakdown was perhaps a little over dramatic, but she was close to breaking point. The repeated attempts at IVF and the latest miscarriage had been wearing for them both. Then there was the continuous pressure from her lecherous boss to hit targets at work. She had come within a whisper of telling him what to do with his job, and that was something that their large mortgage wouldn't allow. Dan's job was no less forgiving and more often than not their evenings ended up with them at each other's throats. She needed a total break, an escape from city life, even if it was only for a paltry weekend.

"Well open the door and come and help me with some of these bags."

They may have been leaving civilization behind, but that didn't mean they couldn't bring a little luxury with them. The back seat heaved with bottles of wine and good food, as well as blankets and duvets. She had made a trip to Harrods food hall especially, wanting to impart a sense of occasion to their getaway.

Shark followed them in to the dusty front room, his nose twitching in disapproval. He set to exploring. It was a plain space, with little more to offer than a wooden table and a couple of chairs. On the wall a faded portrait of a stern old gentleman with a large nose and glazed eyes looked down on them. On the table sat a chipped vase containing the desiccated remains of a bunch of flowers. A circle of dead flies surrounded it. There was also a small stone fireplace. Shadows spread themselves everywhere, painting a haphazard monochrome pattern throughout.

"The lights don't work."

"There's a generator somewhere, remember? Out the back."

Dan sighed but said nothing.

"I bought candles. We can sort the generator out in the morning."

Maria set about finding them while Dan gave her a running commentary as he checked out the rest of their holiday home.

"Something doesn't smell too good in here," he shouted from the kitchen. "Oh. I don't think we'll be using the fridge. I think something died in it."

He came back into the living room before opening another door and vanishing through it.

"Ah, the master bedroom. Not exactly the Ritz but I suppose it'll do. There's a bathroom too. Hmm… it's a little… rural."

Maria giggled. "I'm sure it will be fine. I've found the candles. Let's open a bottle of red."

The candle's faint light was no better than the illumination provided by the full moon. They let it burn anyway, its faint warmth somehow reassuring. Shark settled in under the table and they spent more time listening to his snores than actually talking.

"We can light a fire tomorrow night. He said on the phone that there was a woodpile."

Dan yawned. "That'll be nice honey."

"Come on, we're both exhausted. Let's go to bed."

"Alright. You go on. I'll tidy up here."

Maria stood up and leant over to kiss her husband on

the top of his head.

"Don't be long."

"I won't."

"Good night, Shark."

She headed off into the bedroom and busied herself straightening the bed that Dan had made earlier. Top marks for effort she thought as she arranged it all to meet her own more rigorous standards. Satisfied she went into the bathroom and performed her ablutions. She did her best to ignore the cracked tiles and spots of mould in the corners. When done, she returned to the bedroom, slipped into her nightdress, and got into bed.

"Hurry up, babe," she shouted. There was no response but soon she was drifting in and out of consciousness before falling fully asleep.

Some time later she woke with a start, aware that she was still alone. Looking at her watch she saw that it had been an hour since she came to bed.

"Dan? Dan, where are you?"

Receiving no reply she threw back the two duvets and blanket that covered her. Cursing the chill that enveloped everything beyond the bed, she tiptoed out into the living room. Dan was still at the table, his back to her. The candle had burnt down to nothing and he sat there in the semi-darkness.

"I thought you were coming to bed?"

No reply.

"Come on. What are you doing?"

She walked round the table and frowned when she saw that his eyes were open, staring into the middle distance.

"Dan, are you alright? Dan?"

Maria could see that he was breathing from the rise and fall of his chest; otherwise she might have thought him dead.

"Wake up."

Shark groaned from under the table but Dan didn't react. Feeling panicked she grasped his shoulders and shook. Still nothing. A second attempt was equally ineffective. Without thinking she slapped him. This broke whatever reverie it was that had gripped him and he looked up at her with rheumy eyes.

"What…"

"Jesus, I thought you were having some kind of fit. What the hell?"

"I… I don't know. I was just sitting here and I thought I heard some kind of… some kind of music or something. Well, not exactly music, but some kind of noise out in the forest. I was trying to listen to it and then…"

"Then what?"

He looked thoughtful then shook his head.

"It doesn't matter. I suppose I dozed off."

"You've been out here for an hour. Your eyes were open."

"The drive must have wiped me out. Come on, let's go to bed."

They woke late the next morning. The skies were grey and overcast so they decided to spend the day relaxing and exploring around the cabin. Maria thought that Dan looked a little fazed but decided not to mention it. After lunch he went to fetch some logs, while she flicked through a magazine. She had barely got past the contents page when Shark blustered in, retching and coughing.

"What have you eaten now, Shark?" Maria said, used to his attempts to digest anything new that he happened across.

Shark leant forwards and regurgitated a grey mass. He looked at it then ran back outside, doubtless looking for something more digestible.

"Charming."

She put down her magazine and went to take a closer

look. It was a bundle of fur, straw and what appeared to be tiny bones.

"What the hell?"

"It's a bolus."

The unfamiliar voice made her jump. The speaker was an old man in a crumpled tweed suit and a battered trilby. His face was a mass of overlapping wrinkles out of which sparkled a pair of piercing black eyes. He wore an expression that could have been either a slight sneer or amusement. He bowed as she stared at him, still processing his sudden appearance.

"Sorry. I followed your dog in. It wasn't my intention to startle you. Martin Kelly. We spoke on the phone. The bolus is the vomited remains of an Owl's repast, the unwanted parts. Such fascinating birds, don't you think?"

"I remember dissecting them at school. Not Owls, the er…"

Dan had followed Martin Kelly in, his arms full of logs.

"The bolus. It's a pleasure to meet you. Mr Marshall I presume?"

"You'll excuse me if I don't shake your hand."

"Of course. Let me get out of your way so that you can lighten your load."

Maria shuddered. For some reason she felt nauseous. She had an urge to run outside. There was something about the old man that was deeply repulsive. It was true that he had a certain unpleasant odor about him, an acrid stench that seemed out of place. She noted that his hands were a mass of scratches and his nails long and pointed. Both of these things were unpleasant but shouldn't have been enough to evoke such a strong reaction in her. His voice was reedy, grating, but that was more irritating than anything else. What was wrong with her? Then she saw the way that the man was looking at Dan. At first glance it appeared merely to be polite interest, but she became convinced that there was something predatory about his gaze. She sensed a hunger.

"You'll excuse me for arriving unannounced. I became concerned that you may have become lost on the way here. I wanted to make sure that you were safely… ensconced."

"Well," said Dan, brushing woodchips from his hands, "We did get a little turned around en route but we made it in the end."

"Excellent. We are so happy to have you here. Have you ventured into the forest yet?"

"Not yet. We just thought we'd relax today. I expect we'll explore tomorrow."

"Good. That's very good. Well, I won't keep you any longer. I'll bid you farewell."

"Nice to meet you. Goodbye."

Dan shook Kelly's hand. They both glanced at Maria, who had gone white and was gripping the edge of the table. Martin smiled and left.

"What's the matter with you?"

"I don't know. Didn't you think he was a little strange?"

"He didn't smell fantastic but he seemed alright."

"How did he get here? I didn't hear him arrive. Does he have a car?"

"I don't think so. Didn't see one."

Dan peered out of the door. There was nothing but a vast murmuration of starlings blackening the sky. There was no sign of Martin Kelly.

"Strange. He must have walked through the forest."

"What do you think he meant by we are so happy to have you here?"

"I don't know. Perhaps it was just the royal we."

"He didn't look very royal to me."

"Well, he seemed a little eccentric. I wouldn't worry about it. Come on, the sun is well over the yard arm.

Must be time to crack a bottle and you look like you could use a drink."

Maria woke to the sound of the front door banging in the wind. For a moment she struggled to remember where she was, puzzled by the musty smells and unfamiliar room.

"Dan?"

A sound like the fluttering of wings came from the living room. The door banged again.

"Dan? What the hell are you doing?"

Reluctantly she threw back the covers that they had buried themselves beneath earlier, and got out of bed. The living room was devoid of life.

"Dan? Shark?"

She looked at the front door, now hanging wide open.

"Strange."

As she walked over to peer outside she stood on something other than the cold wooden floor. It was a feather. Absent-mindedly she tickled herself under the chin with it.

There was nothing but an eerie silence outside the cabin. The car was still there, silhouetted under the starless sky. Beyond that, there were just the trees that surrounded them.

"Dan! Shark!" Her voice fell flat in the silence making her feel a little ridiculous. "Where the hell have those two got to?"

Retrieving her coat and fur lined boots she stepped out into the night. The wind was cutting and she wrapped her arms around herself, wishing that she had thought to bring gloves. She walked the cabin's perimeter, noting the woodpile and generator as she passed them. There was no sign of Dan or Shark.

A muffled sound on the wind came from somewhere within the forest. She couldn't identify it but walked towards it anyway. Perhaps Dan had taken Shark out and he had run off. The trees at the edge of the clearing that circled the cabin and their car stood guardian like, shoulder to shoulder. Maria looked up at them, slightly in awe of their size. They dominated the sky, casting long shadows.

"Get a grip, Maria," she told herself. "Dan? Shark?"

As she neared the forest she could definitely hear something moving in the undergrowth. She forced herself to step between the trees and into the darkness beyond. It was dimmer in the forest proper. The moon's light struggled to get past the ceiling of branches. She thought about going back to the car to get the torch from the toolkit, but decided not to bother. Last time she had used it, it hadn't impressed, and she doubted that it would make much difference here.

"Shark?"

There was a loud rustling and something shot out of a nearby bush. It brushed against her legs before disappearing into the darkness. She fell backwards, landing on her backside.

"Shit."

It hadn't been Shark, that was for sure. A fox? A badger? Something else? She liked to think that childhood visits to her grandparents made her a country girl, but she was beginning to doubt herself. Sitting in the dirt, swamped by the damp smell of earth and bush, she felt like a fish out of water. What little calm she had regained since arriving started to evaporate. She staggered to her feet and brushed the muck off her hands. Above, a pair of twinkling golden eyes stared down at her.

Maria walked on through the trees. The forest was full of small sounds that had her looking left and right, but there was nothing. Overhead the branches rustled with some sort of activity but she presumed it to just be the wind.

"Dan! Shark!"

Her voice sounded small and inconsequential now. She wasn't sure what had changed but something definitely had. The branches seemed thicker overhead, and the trunks wider and blacker than before. Clouds drifted across the moon, plunging her into intermittent darkness. The temperature had dropped and she could see her breath condensing before her.

The faint jingling sound of a dog's collar reached her ears, along with what she imagined to be a distant whining. Both were somewhat indistinct but enough to spur her on to a quickened pace. The thought of seeing Shark cheered her somewhat. Truth be told, he was a kind of surrogate child to her and Dan, ludicrous as that might be. He was 120 pounds of muscle and slightly dim, but they loved him nonetheless. Dan had wanted to call him Jaws because of his penchant for tearing things to shreds but somehow they had ended up with Shark. Details of the negotiations were lost in a haze of time and alcohol, but Shark he was.

Pushing on through a flurry of stinging low plants bought her to a clearing where the trees were a little further apart. In the centre was an elderly stump, all splintered and split. As she approached, she realized that there was something resting on it, something familiar. Her heart sank as her initial suspicion was confirmed. It was Shark's thick leather collar. At that moment she heard the first owl.

Its screeching hoot increased in volume as the creature descended down towards her. Before she had a chance to turn, its claws tore into the flesh on the back of her neck. Its screaming cry sounded like laughter as it returned to its perch. She saw the second bird as it attacked from the front. With its wings outstretched it seemed huge. The impact sent her sprawling for the second time that evening. She screamed as talons tore through her clothes and into her chest. A sharp beak scratched one side of her face and then the other, cutting deep tracks into her cheeks. Flailing wildly, one hand still holding the collar, she beat it away before scrambling back upright.

As her tears mixed with the blood on her face, she ran. Her heart thumped and skipped, and her head throbbed with shock. She could hardly believe what had just happened. A part of her tried to reason that there was no way that it could have, that it must have been some kind of dream or hallucination. As much as she would have loved to embrace that thought she pushed it aside. Her wounds were evidence enough that it had been real. Perhaps the birds had been nesting. The parental instinct could provoke extreme reactions in wild animals. That made a certain amount of sense but what was Shark's collar doing there?

"I need to get back to the cabin. Everything will be alright if I just go back to the cabin."

She span around, trying to get her bearings. She had only a vague sense of the direction in which she had come, and she didn't want to see the owls again. Judging by the position of the moon in the sky she thought that perhaps she could navigate round the clearing and make her way back.

"Come on, Maria. You can do this."

She had taken no more than two steps when there was a flurry of wings and an owl swooped down at her again. It glanced off her shoulder as she turned to go back in the direction that she had come from. As she passed her starting point another bird came at her, screeching malevolently. She ducked and its talons scraped across the top of her head, pulling out a clump of hair as it went. It was then that she noticed the eyes.

There were dozens of them, perhaps hundreds, glinting in the moonlight, scattered amongst the branches of the trees. She felt her knees weaken as a sense of unreality came over her again. For a split second she wondered once more if it was all an elaborate dream. More than that, she hoped that it was a dream. There was no waking up from this though. No amount of blinking or pinching herself was going to bring it to an end. The pain from her wounds was still there, as was the blood on her hands. Even so, her mind reeled as it tried to get to grips with a nightmare reality that seemed tenuous at best.

Maria began to walk, cowering under their gaze. Every sound made her twitch, wary that they would attack again. She was cold and the gouges across her cheeks pulsed with every heartbeat. The damage to her chest felt serious but she didn't dare look too closely.

After an eternity the forest thinned and she found herself in another clearing. At its centre was a peculiar stone shack. It had a square base and a domed roof. Wind and rain had rounded the haphazard bricks at their edges. Clearly it had been there for a very long time. What caught her attention though were the owls that covered it, as well as the surrounding grass. They were everywhere, strutting back and forth, preening themselves or sitting as if waiting for her arrival. When she came out of the tree line they all turned to look at her.

In front of the building was a particularly thick mob of birds. As she walked towards them they hopped and flew away, revealing what had caught their interest.

"No..."

She broke into a run and fell to her knees in front of the mutilated remains of what had once been Shark. Most of his head remained, although one eye and most of the lips had been pecked away. The rest of the body was little more than a skeleton with only a few shreds of torn flesh remaining. It sat in a foul circle of gore and offal.

"Oh Shark. My baby..."

Fury filled her and she turned to confront the birds.

"You bastards! Why did you do this, why? Where is my husband?"

A visible ripple of doubt and hesitancy ran through her feathered audience. For a moment Maria thought she had actually scared them. It was a fleeting sensation though and they quickly recovered from their surprise, moving in towards her. With a slow determination they pushed her towards the door of the stone shack. Still shaking with anger she had little choice but to step inside.

Her nose filled with a putrid miasma that made her gag. The room smelled of death and decay. As her eyes became used to the darkness she saw that the floor was littered with bones of all sizes. An indecipherable arcane scrawl covered the walls. Her attention turned to the far end of the space.

The entire back wall was an altar of some kind, constructed from the same stones as the rest of the building. On top of it a plethora of skulls had been arranged in ascending sizes, ranging from rodent to human. In front of them lay a sword, long and rusty with a black patina speckling the blade. Two extended claws formed the guard, while the pommel was an owl's head.

From the swirling shadows emerged a kneeling figure before the altar. Squinting in the darkness she managed to make out a familiar dressing gown and pajamas.

"Dan? Dan, is that you? Thank God..."

She stumbled forwards to greet him, desperate to embrace him. His simple presence seemed to ease some of the horror that surrounded her, and tears of relief rolled down her face. Maria watched as he stood and turned, her arms outstretched, willing him to come to her.

"Oh Dan..."

As his features caught the little moonlight that was in the room, she felt her intestines turn to water. Where once there had been cool blue eyes, there was a pair of glistening golden spheres that burned into her with their glance. A sharp curving beak sat where there should have been a sturdy nose and strong smiling mouth. Instead of words of comfort there came only a terrible shriek that tore through her eardrums.

"What did they do to you?" she screamed.

There was no reply that she could understand. Instead he snatched up the sword and took a step towards her, gripping it two handed. He swung it, narrowly missing her chest. She screamed and scurried back, bones scrunching under foot.

"Get away from me."

The next swing slashed across her arm, cutting through her coat and into flesh. Blood seeped down, soaking the material. He followed it up with a jab that struck the soft skin of her belly. Maria yelped in pain and looked around her for an exit but there was none. A wall of birds blocked the door and she would never fit through the narrow windows.

"Dan, it's me. Maria. I'm your wife. Remember?"

Another jab of the sword suggested that he didn't and she fell back against the wall clutching her midriff. As the warm sticky fluid flowed through her fingers, she watched a transformation come over what had once been Dan. His clothes split and fell away as his limbs expanded and became feathered. His head merged down into his body and claws stretched out from his feet. The sword clattered to the ground as his hands merged with rapidly forming wings. Maria slid to the floor, barely enough energy left within her to keep her eyes open.

"Let me go now Dan. Let me go…"

The creature that she had once loved strutted back and forth, the last vestiges of his former self washed away by the ancient evil that rested in this place. There was no mercy forthcoming, nor was there any hope in that avian face. Her part in the rebirth of this past shade was complete and so her time was over. A crimson stream rose up to choke her as the room filled with feathered white, a storm of tearing claws and shredding beaks. As her eyes fluttered and then closed, the last thing she saw was Dan, being absorbed by the tornado of owls, forever more a part of the bitter parliament.

CHARLIE'S TURN

"Quiet now. Not a sound."

Charlie looked at his brother, doubt weighing heavily on his mind. He shivered in the forest shadow, wishing they could go back into the sunshine. Brendan was in one of his moods though, and he knew from experience that it was best just to do whatever he was told or risk a beating.

The rabbit was blissfully unaware of their presence. It sat in the middle of a dappled clearing, attention focused on making a feast of the fresh grass. Brendan dropped down to his knees and gestured that Charlie do the same. The ground was cold and wet. Charlie watched as his sibling readied the wooden catapult that he had pleaded with Danny Smith to borrow. No doubt it had come with a price to be exacted at a later time.

Time slowed to a crawl as the stone arced away from them towards their prey. It was a perfect shot, a dream shot even, and for a second they were frozen in wonder as they watched it hit the target with a thud. Then everything sped up again, and Brendan was on his feet and running. Shoving the catapult into his back pocket, he grabbed the dazed rabbit and held it up by its ears. It twitched feebly in his grasp.

"Did you see that, Charlie? Did you see?"

Charlie shuffled his feet and nodded. He just wanted it to stop now. He wished he was playing football, or listening to his mother sing while she washed the dishes.

"Watch this."

Charlie stared wide-eyed as Brendan produced a penknife and slid the blade across the twitching animal's throat. A terrible screech filled the air and then silence returned. With legs like lead he marched over to take a closer look, driven by some overwhelming inner curiosity.

"You killed it."

"Of course I killed it. That's what you're meant to do. It'll be your turn next. We're hunters now. Come on."

They ran through the trees, whooping as they went, finally bursting out into the cornfield that ran along the forest's west side. The field was all blackened stubble, the annual burning having taken place a few days earlier. Charlie smiled as the heat of the sun warmed them. Arms outstretched, he lifted his face to the sky and shuddered, the chill of the forest evaporating.

He looked at the rabbit. Removed from the arboreal gloom, death had somehow made it less real. How could this ragged bunch of fur have ever been a living thing?

Brendan was the first to see the plane. It appeared over the horizon, beyond the dips and curves of the Kent countryside. They could see smoke pouring from the wings as it approached, engines spluttering and whining.

"It's a bomber." Brendan jumped up and down with excitement, his bloody prize forgotten. He dropped the limp carcass so he could shield his eyes to better focus.

"I want to go home now."

Brendan glanced at his brother, frowned, and then turned away.

"Look! It's Germans. It's a bloody German bomber."

Charlie didn't like it when Brendan used what he called 'daddy words'. They made him uncomfortable.

"Take me home, Brendan. I want to go home."

As the plane got closer, they could see flames licking around the fuselage. It was clearly in serious trouble. Both boys stared up as it passed several hundred feet overhead. They gasped in unison as a man suddenly fell from the ailing craft and plummeted towards the forest. A partially unraveled parachute streamed out behind him, too late to save him from the verdant grasp of the trees.

Neither of the boys were watching as the stricken Heinkel vanished over the horizon behind them, nor did they hear the explosion, or see the distant plume of smoke that marked where it had hit the ground. They were standing like statues, temporarily immobilized as their young minds grappled with what had happened.

"Come on!"

Brendan sprinted towards the tree line and then stopped when he realised that Charlie wasn't following him.

"Come on! Now!" The last word was a command, spoken with the innate authority of the elder. It couldn't be disobeyed, certainly not by a five year old. Charlie reluctantly trotted after his sibling.

The forest seemed darker than it had before. Everything about it had become more visceral, more intrusive on the senses than it had been only five minutes earlier. The smell of bark and mud was overwhelming. Birds that had been conspicuous only by their absence during the rabbit hunt were suddenly squawking out in alarm and discontent. A fox streaked across their path and disappeared into the undergrowth.

It was ten minutes before they found the airman, though it felt more like hours. His parachute was spread across the old tree above where he lay, the silk shredded by its branches. He was in a bad way. His flight suit was torn and burnt, covered with black and crimson streaks. A white nub of bone protruded from his right leg. He turned his head slowly towards the sound of the boys approaching. His eyes were piercing blue. He smiled weakly through blood splashed lips.

"*Kinder.*"

"Look Charlie, a real German."

Brendan whipped his catapult out and fired a stone at the man before his brother could manage a reply. It struck his eye with a sickly thump. The German screamed and put his hands over the new wound. A stream of blood flowed out from between his fingers.

Charlie frowned and looked at his feet. At five, the world was still full of surprises and he was quite used to being confronted by new situations. For all he knew, burnt Nazis falling from aeroplanes were fair game to passing hunters like he and Brendan.

"Your turn."

His brother was holding out the little knife towards him. A spark of sunlight reflected off it, making it gleam in Brendan's dirty upturned palm. Charlie looked at the knife, then at his brother, and finally at the injured airman.

"Your turn, Charlie."

PATER IN TENEBRIS

Even before I inspected the wound, I knew that it was bad news. It wasn't particularly deep but I could feel the infection taking hold. I felt dirty. I rummaged through several drawers before finding the testing kit. It was buried under a pile of papers, hidden away in the hope that it would never be needed. I ripped open the packaging and jammed the needle into a vein. The barrel filled with my blood and I pulled the rig free. Specks of crimson covered the kitchen table as I squeezed the syringe's contents out onto the blotter. The chemically-infused paper turned a deep blue. According to the result card there was just under an hour before I became one of them.

How could I have been so stupid? I used to be meticulously careful, but routine had made me careless. Three of them were hovering around the door when I came out of the deserted grocery store. I took care of the first with the pistol in my right hand. At such a short range, his head had disintegrated. My machete was in my other hand, and I swung at the second's neck. It sliced through the creature's rotting flesh with ease, decapitating it with one blow. I took a step back and aimed at the third. As I fired, it lunged. My shot still took off the top of his skull, but as he fell his teeth scraped against my hand. That was all it took.

My mind reeled as I instinctively looked for someone to blame. Of course there was nobody else to put that burden on. It was entirely my fault, and it was childish of me to think otherwise, but that's the way the human mind works. It's all about protecting the ego. Once I'd accepted responsibility, my thoughts turned to finding help. Again, there was nobody to turn to. A vision of my dead parents, out in the night looking for meat, came to me. They were lost, and now so was I. It was tempting to just fall into self-pity. The shadow of death pushed down on me, darkening my thoughts and attempting to drown me in despair. I didn't have time for that.

After checking that all the locks and bolts were in place, I went upstairs. My family was enjoying that one part of the day that could, with luck, be entirely blissful. They were asleep. My first stop was the children's room. I sat on the floor between their two beds listening to the sweet sound of my son snoring. He was seven years old. How could I expect him to take over as man of the house? My four-year old daughter slept silently with a huge smile on her face.

It had been a long time since I'd been able to hit the sack with any expectation of real rest. The frothing world of insanity just beyond our garden wall kept me tossing and turning. Nightmares were what I expected, and nightmares were what I got. None of that mattered to little Natalie though. Her dreams were still untouched by the horror outside. My wife had been pregnant when the virus crushed civilization, so this artificial haven was all our daughter had ever known. Shielding the children from the monsters at the gate was our number one priority. In all honesty, it was what kept us sane. Focusing on their needs helped us forget our own problems. It may have been an illusion but it had been an effective one. They had lived decent lives up until now.

Until now. Now the game changed. It was one thing having two parents to look after you, but how could my wife maintain the pretense on her own? She was incredibly capable, and with effort she could find supplies and keep the wolf from the door, but it would be an endless struggle. The kids would have to stay at home on their own, and if something happened while she was out… it didn't bear thinking about. There was suddenly no doubt in my mind that something terrible would happen, and probably sooner rather than later.

I had always hunted and kept guns. It was something that my father taught me. Even with this enthusiasm for the tools of the trade, staying alive had remained a close run thing. Eleanor detested them and would have the odds against her from the very first time that she entered the killing grounds. It seemed so incredibly unfair that one slip on my behalf should ruin their lives.

I tried to think of options, but it was hopeless. As far as we know, there were no other survivors. We hadn't seen or heard anything since Natalie was born. The world had gone quiet; nobody was going to come to our rescue. We considered a road trip, but it seemed suicidal when one considered the millions of ravenous infected surrounding us.

One thought kept coming back to me, and I kept trying to push it away. I had to somehow shield them from being killed horribly or living in constant fear and then being killed horribly. I could only think of one possible option that would save them from that fate.

I got to my feet and pulled myself together. In a way, I felt relieved to have a sense of purpose. With so little time left, I needed to do the right thing for my family. Nothing else mattered. I wasn't entirely without doubt though. Seeing one's own child come into the world is not something you ever forget. My two had come surfing out in a coat of vernix and blood, eager to suck in their first breath. I'd cut the cord and held them in my arms during the first few moments of separation. After that came all of the other wonders that parenthood bestows on you. Walking, talking, becoming… watching my children learning to be was probably the only thing I considered to be worth a damn in my whole stupid life. When you have kids, you can't help but wonder what they will be like as they get older. Your imagination takes you to odd places the first time you see that little version of yourself. Could I really murder that dream and all of its possibilities?

Twenty minutes had passed since I went upstairs. I had to keep moving. I kissed both of them gently on the cheek. Natalie stirred.

"Daddy?"

"Yes, it's just me. Go back to sleep honey."

"Are you okay, Daddy?"

"I'm fine, everything's fine."

I stroked her head until her breathing switched into that slow rhythm that indicated she was back in the land of nod. Another five minutes had passed. I went out into the corridor.

My wife was snoring gently in our bedroom. Like mother, like son. Even now, the sound made me smile. Why she had selected me to spend her life with was mystifying. She was smart, funny and beautiful, and could have done much better for herself. It was so tempting to wake her up. We discussed everything. I loved talking to her. The problem was, I knew how the conversation would go, and I just couldn't face it. She wasn't going to be able to conjure up some magical cure for my inevitable fate. She also wasn't going to be able to process the concept of murder-suicide being the best option. Human nature would overcome logic, and we'd end up going round and round in circles until it was too late. The only gift that my damnation had given me was clarity, and it wasn't something I could share. I didn't have time to argue the point.

Not daring to even look at her, I came back down the stairs. Just over half an hour remaining. My legs were starting to feel stiff, and I had shooting pains running up and down my spine. A strong taste of salt filled my mouth. At this rate I could have less time than I previously thought.

My mood deteriorated as I set to work. While I hauled a barrel of heating oil into the front room, I was thinking about all the books that I could never read. I had shelves of them, waiting for me to find the time to indulge. As I dragged boxes of ammunition out of the cellar I cursed my own lack of religious faith. Any childhood notion of there being a heaven had left me as the world turned into a living hell. It would have been nice to imagine that I was sending my family to a better place. Still, there was no time for pleasantry or fantasizing.

I was about to begin pouring the oil over the living room when a small voice interrupted me.

"Daddy, what are you doing?"

It was Natalie. She was clutching her bear and looking at me doubtfully. Her eyes were full of sleep. My heart twisted in my chest.

"Nothing darling. Don't worry. Just go back to sleep."

"You don't look well, Daddy."

"I'm fine. Please go back to bed."

"Your voice sounds funny."

I really wanted her to go away. A part of me wanted to pick her up and hug her but another wanted to shake her until she understood. Time was running out and I didn't trust myself anymore.

"Is it the morning?"

Bobby had come down the stairs. Fury washed over me. It was so strong, that for a moment I thought my knees were going to give way beneath me. I tried to focus and push it back.

"Please go to bed." My voice was a whisper.

It was getting hard to think clearly. I needed them out of the way or I was going to lose impetus.

"Daddy, what are you doing with that barrel? It smells horrible."

I looked at the oil, suddenly aware of the fumes filling the room. A terrible image of my children in flames flashed before me.

"Yes. What exactly are you doing?"

All of the commotion had woken my wife. She stood there in her dressing gown, trying to make sense of the scene in front of her. The loaded pistol that we kept in the bedroom was in her hand.

"I…"

"Jesus, your eyes are yellow. You look…"

The color drained from her face as realization hit her.

"Kids, go to bed now!"

"But Mummy…"

"Now!"

Reluctantly they made their way up the stairs. I watched them go, my anger from a few moments before replaced by a deep sadness.

"What the hell happened?"

"One of them bit me. It was an accident. I…"

A single tear rolling down her cheek stopped me in my tracks. The world went into slow motion as I watched it descend. It's movement and the trail that it left on her cheek captivated me. My attention turned to her skin and her lips. She was beautiful but the urges that were rising within me were confused. I wanted to kiss her, to make love to her, but I also felt hunger of another kind. I could smell her body, her flesh. It called to me and I took a step towards her.

"Stay there."

The gun was in front of her, pointing straight at my heart. I looked at it, and then her, confused by the juxtaposition.

"Why is there ammo all over the place? What the hell are you doing?"

I dragged my attention back to reality.

"In less than twenty minutes, I'm going to be one of them. I didn't want to leave you alone. I didn't want…"

"What? You were going to kill us."

"It was for your own good. I didn't want you to suffer."

"You didn't want us to suffer? Did you think about what I might have wanted? Why didn't you wake me up? Christ…"

My head felt like it was going to explode.

"I'm sorry…"

"Sorry? Oh God."

My fingers twitched of their own accord. A shudder ran through me. There was a low droning tone in my ears.

"I love you, you know." My voice seemed to be coming from another room.

"I love you too."

As I looked at her face my vision flickered. It was like watching an old film with random frames spliced into it. I could see her when we first met, when we first made love. For a split second I was seeing her eyes as I passed Bobby to her just after he was born. Time slipped.

"So what happens now?"

I had no words. I wanted so much for there to be more time. I wanted to see my children turn into adults. I wanted to grow old and watch the sunset. None of this was going to happen. I could feel my veins hardening and my blood thickening.

"You were going to kill us?"

"I love you too."

"You don't look well Daddy."

I fell back against the wall. My wife had become nothing more than a blurred vision somewhere in front of me. I wanted to reach out and grab her, but my limbs were like lead. Nothing felt right. An inhuman groan oozed out of me.

"You're going to have to go outside."

I felt the pain in her voice.

"You were going to kill us."

"Daddy, what are you doing?"

It took all of my will, but I had one more thing to say to the woman I loved.

"Kill me. Kill me now."

For a moment I thought I was back in my children's room, sitting on the floor. I could hear the soft sounds of their breathing as they slept.

"Jesus. Your eyes are yellow."

"Your voice sounds funny."

"You're going to have to go outside." My wife's voice cracked as she spoke. "You can't stay here."

"Kill me."

"I can't, my love, I really can't."

An inhuman howl echoed around my head. I knew it had come from me, but I was drifting away from myself, losing control. I was barely aware that I was moving. Somewhere locks were being undone. A door clicked open. I was getting wet. Rain.

"I'm sorry, darling. I love you."

A door slammed shut. I was stumbling away from the house, but not of my own volition. I felt like a passenger in my own body. I was vaguely aware of shadows and flashes of light but it was all too abstract to resolve into a solid image.

"Are you OK, Daddy?"

My daughter's face flashed before me. I wanted to pick her up but I couldn't. She disappeared.

"I'm sorry darling, I love you."

I span around clumsily. My wife wasn't there. In fact, I had no idea where I was. I had only been in the dark for five minutes but it seemed like an eternity. Where was my house? Where was my family? An awful smell filled my nostrils, the not-unfamiliar stink of the animated dead. They swarmed out of the night, jostling against me and filling the air with their moaning. I was travelling with them now, lost and hungry. I could taste the dried remains of my last meal rotting on my lips, but I didn't remember eating. Surely I had been inside only moments before.

"Daddy, what are you doing?"

MILKSHAKE

"Gideon, take the boy's bag. I'm going to show him around."

Louis watched as his cousin snatched his pack and loped off towards the tumbledown farmhouse. He felt a pang of doubt as all of his possessions in the world disappeared into the distance.

"I was sorry to hear about your Pa, boy. We were never close since he ran off to the city, but he was kin."

His Uncle put a chubby hand on his shoulder.

"Still, we're kin too so at least you ain't alone in the world. That's a good thing, right boy?"

Louis looked up at his Uncle and nodded doubtfully. In fact, he found it hard to believe that they were related at all. Louis was slight, while his Uncle was a bald giant of a man. Where Louis was all cheekbones and pale skin, Uncle Moses was the proud owner of a fat face, reddened by the burst blood vessels of a seasoned drinker. Moses scrutinized him with his small, black piggy eyes before breaking into a smile.

"I heard your Pa was killed by a junkie. Blew his head clean off."

He squeezed Louis' shoulder so hard it hurt.

"Good news is, we don't get any of those crazies up here. We're living the dream here, boy."

"That's good," mumbled Louis.

"Of course it is. Come on; let's go take a look at the workings. I think you're going to be impressed, boy. We got it going on. We'd better hurry though. I think your Aunt is cooking us up something special."

Louis followed his Uncle across the muddy yard towards a huge barn. It had no windows and the only entrance was padlocked shut. Moses pulled a bunch of keys from the pocket of his overalls and unlocked it.

"Always keep this door closed, boy. We don't want the livestock runnin' all over the place."

He beckoned for his nephew to go in. Louis found himself in a dark room full of cutting tools. From the walls hung machetes, chainsaws, axes and a cornucopia of other sharp steel implements that he couldn't name. When Moses flicked the switch on behind him, they gleamed under the neon strip light.

"I like to keep my toys clean."

Louis looked at the workbench that ran along the far wall. It was piled up with rusting tins of nameless cleaning products and darkly stained towels.

"Gideon likes to earn himself a few extra bucks giving them a shine. I'll say this for the boy, he may be as dumb as a bucket of bricks, but he does a fine job. Of course, I do all the grinding myself."

He pointed to a machine under the bench that Louis hadn't noticed.

"Maybe you'd like to learn to do that one day?"

"Maybe," he muttered, seeing his future flushing away.

"Come on. Let's go feed the swine."

The door to the next room was locked with an electronic keypad. Moses prodded it several times before getting the combination right. It opened with a resounding click.

A foul stench hit them as they walked in. Louis grimaced and held his nose. His Uncle roared with laughter.

"Oh, you'll get used to that. It can't be helped. Damn porkers rolling around in their own… well, you know."

Louis walked over to the pens and looked in over the low wall. His mind did a momentary flip as it attempted to resolve what he had expected to see, with what it actually did. There, rolling in the filth, were four obese and naked humans. He looked back at his Uncle and then back at the pen.

"Beautiful, ain't they? Not much longer and they'll be done. Here, give them something to eat."

Moses scooped up a pail of swill and handed it to him. Louis took it with shaking hands and approached the pen.

"Be careful now. They'll bite."

Louis threw the contents in and backed off as quickly as he could. One of the three males, a heavily bearded bear of a man, leapt for the food. The wild haired female crawled forwards and smashed him in the face with a clenched fist. She was enormous and his nose collapsed into a pulp of bone and blood. He retreated to the back of the pen where the other two males were waiting patiently for their turn to feed. Moses roared with laughter.

"Guess we know who's boss, eh son?"

Louis didn't look at him. He was transfixed. His thoughts were in turmoil. It was true to say that he was a city boy, born and bred amidst concrete and tarmac. He'd never been to a farm in his life, but this wasn't what he had expected. The logical part of his brain knew very well that this was an abomination, but what did that make his Uncle? It was impossible to think clearly while this mass of white muddy flesh was quivering in front of him. She looked up at him and shrieked before sticking her face back into her meal.

"Let's move on."

Moses grabbed Louis' arm and steered him through the thick hanging sheets that separated this area from the next. It was noticeably colder here. Louis looked around him and felt his knees began to buckle.

"Now boy, this is where we hang the meat and do our butchering."

Six corpses were hanging from the ceiling. A couple of them were hanging from chains attached to their feet. The rest were suspended by meat hooks that pierced their backs. One had been completely skinned; another was missing both legs. Louis' gaze flicked back and forth, cataloguing the horrors that had been inflicted on them.

"So we've got a couple of porkers in here."

Moses shoved an older looking man whose chest had been split wide open. "This one was a travelling salesman. Thought he'd fool us; thought we were simple because we live out in the country."

A look of anger flashed across his face before it returned to its normal sedate state. He pushed another couple of bodies, and they swung back and forth on their hooks.

"Picked these ones up out on the highway. Hitchhikers. Of course, that wild free-range stuff will never be as good as farm fed, but some people like it. The boy put up a bit of a fight, but your Aunt soon put paid to that. It don't pay to mess with your Aunt, let me tell you."

He smiled an avuncular smile and a beatific expression crossed his face.

"Damn, but I love that woman."

The world was spinning around Louis. The grimacing faces of the refrigerated dead zoomed in and out of focus. He felt like his skull was going to explode. He stumbled and grasped at the only thing available for support, which was his Uncle.

"Hell boy, you alright? Damn, what was I thinking? You must be exhausted from all that travelling and here's me going on and on. It's cold in here too. Come on, tour's nearly over."

Louis felt himself propelled through the flesh forest and passed another set of thick separators. The temperature rose a notch and he took a deep breath of the warmer air. It smelled of straw and sweat. Elevator music played softly from hidden speakers. The room was brightly lit. The righthand side of the room was divided into half a dozen high walled stalls.

"We like to keep things nice in here. I like my girls to be happy. Keeps the milk sweet."

Moses beamed with pride.

"There's some say that there's no money in dairy these days, but my customers would tell you different."

He shoved Louis towards the stalls.

"Now go take a look."

Louis looked into the first stall, willing it to contain a cow. It did not. Instead he saw a filthy mattress onto which was chained a heavily pregnant woman. Four manacles connected her arms and legs to concrete posts. She was half dressed in a ripped sheet that barely kept her decent. He estimated that she wasn't much older than him. Nineteen perhaps. She was pretty too he thought, even though her blue eyes were unfocused and heavy with sleep.

"We keep 'em sedated. They're happier that way."

As he stood there, she looked in his direction and seemed to be trying to make sense of what she was seeing. She lifted an arm to point at him before letting it drop back down. With feet of lead he walked to the next stall. The picture was the same. Another girl of a similar age, long blond hair instead of brown and curly, the same disconnected look on her face.

"This here is May. She's my champion milker. I tell you, you haven't tasted anything until you've had a milkshake from May."

May noticed Louis and Moses for the first time. Her lips moved as if she was trying to say something, but nothing could be heard. A small stream of saliva ran down from the edge of her mouth.

"I let Gideon do most of the milking. He seems to enjoy his work. Say boy, you want to have a go? See how a real farm hand works?"

Louis turned to his Uncle. There was a white noise building in his head now, drowning out all logical thought. His hands were shaking.

"You… you…"

His voice sounded like it was coming from somewhere far away.

"Do you catch pregnant women? That's…"

Moses clapped his hands together and shook his head.

"Hell no. Now that just wouldn't be right. We take care of all the sperminating here."

"You mean you…"

His Uncle looked sheepish.

"Me? Holy Jesus, your Aunt would chop my… No, sir. Gideon takes care of that. If you like you could help him out."

Louis felt like the world was falling from under him.

"What about the babies? What happens to the babies?"

For once Moses had nothing to say. He folded his arms and just looked at his nephew quizzically. The twinkle in his eyes seemed to have been replaced by something dark, something that finally made sense to Louis. Louis ran. He burst through into the cold room, blindly bumping into the hanging corpses as he went. He could hear his Uncle shouting.

"Hey boy, boy! You all right? What's the matter?"

He burst into the swine room. His heart was in his throat. One of the males had mounted the female and roared an inhuman sound of warning as he passed. The door to the tool room was open and he hurried in. Without thinking he grabbed a short double-sided axe with a stout wooden handle from the wall and ran outside. As he came into the yard, he almost knocked his cousin over, only just managing to bring himself to a stop before making contact.

"Where are you goin', cuz?" said Gideon.

Louis took a step back and gripped the axe.

"Get away from me."

Gideon grinned showing teeth that were uneven and chipped at the edges.

"Now what's gotten into you?"

He took a pace forwards, narrowing the gap between the two boys.

Louis swung the axe towards him, but his cousin was surprisingly agile, given his size, and dodged the blow. He swung again but missed.

"You crazy or what? I'm going to give you such a beating, city boy."

This time the axe made contact, wedging itself into Gideon's neck. Arterial blood gushed out from the wound and he swayed unsteadily for a moment before slamming onto the floor. Louis looked down at him for a moment, watching him die, before remembering that his Uncle was probably only moments behind him. Looking around he could see nowhere to hide. There was only the house. Perhaps he could find his bag and make a run for it.

The front door opened with a loud squeak and he found himself in a musty hallway. A couple of bad reproduction paintings hung from the walls that were decorated with peeling wallpaper. It smelled of urine.

"Is that my boys?" came a woman's voice from somewhere further inside.

He looked around for an escape route, unsure which direction the sound had come from. Wishing he hadn't left the axe outside, he went into the nearest room. It was a poor choice. He had never seen his Aunt before. She was an imposing sight. The floral print dress she was wearing struggled to contain a body that must have weighed at least three hundred pounds. Her facial features were pinched and simian.

"Why you must be Louis. Welcome to the farm. I was sorry to hear about your Pa. That's tough, what with you having no Momma and all."

She turned and pulled a large baking tray from the range.

"This'll raise your spirits."

The smell of pork filled the room and despite himself Louis felt his mouth water. She slammed the tray down on the splintered dining table in the centre of the room. Without thinking he looked down at the contents of the tray. The baby had been wrapped in a bacon shroud before cooking. Although its crispy little face no longer had eyes, he felt caught by its sightless gaze. He really wanted to turn away but found it impossible. He was still staring as his Uncle stepped up behind him and cut off his head.

NOSE TO THE WINDOW

"And as cities across the world continue to burn, scientists confirm that the anomaly is still expanding. Although various theories have been put forward, most experts agree that…"

A burst of static drowned out the announcer. Greg shrugged and turned the dial until he found a music station. Soft rock filled the cab of his pickup and he drummed along with his fingers on the steering wheel. Reception was terrible but he wasn't bothered.

There hadn't been any other cars on the road for at least an hour. Outside there was nothing but the desert, nothing but scrub stretching out as far as the rocky outcrops in the distance. Up in the cold night sky the light from the stars was blurred and peculiar where it should have been crisp and clear. 'Gravitational distortion,' one of the supposed experts on the radio had said, whatever that meant.

"Daddy?"

"Honey?"

He turned the volume down and glanced over his shoulder at the back seat. Only his daughter's head showed from under the pile of blankets. Her eyes were half closed and her voice had the wrinkle of someone who wasn't properly awake.

"Where are we going?"

It must have been getting on for two when he'd stubbed out his cigarette and abandoned his rocking chair on the verandah. He'd been half asleep, listening to the world implode, when inspiration had hit.

"Just a road trip honey. I didn't want to wake you so I wrapped you all up and popped you in the back there."

"Where are we going?"

"Well… I reckon we'll go and pay your mother a visit and then we'll go to the beach."

"Oh good. I like the beach…"

Even though it was only a couple of seconds before he turned to smile at her, she had already returned to the land of dreams. He turned the radio off so that he could hear her gentle snoring as he drove. It was her that he felt most sorry for. He struggled to be particularly horrified by the potential end of the world or his own demise. It was odd but getting older had smoothed out the fury and expectation that he had been guilty of as a young man. There was a time when he would have raged against the injustice of it all but he had lost too much already. Apart from the love that he felt for his daughter, he was simply past caring.

"Damn…"

Lost in his thoughts he had almost hit the black shape lying across the highway. He wrenched the wheel to the right, taking them bumping over the ragged verge. With a squeal of tires he dragged them back onto the asphalt and stopped.

"Stay here honey."

The shotgun felt cold in his grip as he got out to investigate. It was clear now that the shape was a person, a large male person, lying unconscious in the road.

"How are you doing there buddy? You chose a hell of a place for a rest. I nearly made it permanent."

His new acquaintance didn't respond. Greg wondered if he was dead. Pointing the gun at him, he approached. The smell of alcohol filled his nostrils and he shook his head.

"Getting blind drunk I can understand. Doing it out here… not so much."

He poked the man with the edge of his foot.

"Hey!"

Getting no response he walked back to the truck and put the gun on the flatbed. He returned to the man and took a deep breath before grabbing his hands.

"Sorry man, I'd have given you a lift into town but there's no way I'm going to be able to lift you up. If you freeze to death, I apologise in advance."

Once the drunk was hauled safely off the road he retrieved his gun and got back into the cab. Zoe was still asleep. Thankful for small mercies he got back under way.

He regretted his decision to go through Albermal almost immediately. It wouldn't have been a huge inconvenience to go off road and avoid it but he hadn't thought it worthwhile. Now he wasn't so sure. A crowd was milling around outside the town's only drinking hole and they looked drunk and ornery. A couple of sleepers, or corpses, it was impossible to be sure, littered the sidewalk. Around them stumbled the still upright, their dazed expressions pale under the moonlight. A few of them were exchanging punches, engaged in a halfhearted fight that seemed to be happening in slow motion. One of the others staggered out into the road. Greg eased off the gas, his eyes fixed on the way ahead. Carefully he steered the truck around the man. He was aware of muted rock and roll drifting out from the bar. The song was unfamiliar.

"Easy now, Mister. Just passing by."

As he passed, the drunk stumbled into the side of the truck and banged his fists against the window.

"What are you going to do? What are you going to do?"

Greg sped up and watched him fall onto the asphalt

in the rear view mirror. He was happy to see that the incident had passed Zoe by.

At the other end of the street was the only other show in town. Like the bar, there was a crowd of regulars swarming around the church. Unlike the bewildered patrons at the Eagle Tavern though, these people looked focused and angry. An unnatural orange glow flickered from inside the building.

"What's going on, Daddy?"

Zoe had pulled herself upright, pressing her nose up against the window. Greg was about to respond when the double doors burst open accompanied by a cloud of black smoke. Three people emerged, one of them a priest, clearly being dragged out by the other two.

"What are they doing, Daddy?"

Greg's first thought was that he was looking at a rescue but there was something about the scene that didn't add up. His eyes moved from the wide-eyed fear on the holy man's face to the crazed fury in the expressions of those around him. There was something wild, an intangible wrongness that enveloped the whole scene. He watched as a young woman stuck her face up close to the terrified priest. It was impossible to hear what she was saying but judging by the spittle on her lips and her balled fists, it was nothing good.

"Daddy, what are they going to do to that man?"

"I don't know honey. I think they're rescuing him. The church is on fire."

For a split second his gaze locked with the priest's. His expression reminded Greg of his time in-country with the Infantry. Most people would never feel that level of desperation, never find themselves staring death in the face. Now he knew that he had lied to his daughter.

"I'm not sure though, darling. It's…"

The priest had broken free of his captors and was running towards them. They were still rolling and Greg was tempted to put the pedal to the metal. This wasn't his circus to get involved in. Zoe was watching, her mouth wide open now, both palms flat against the truck window.

"Run!" she screamed.

"Ah hell."

Greg slowed a little more and pulled his shotgun from the passenger seat. He stuck it out of the window.

"You, get in the back. The rest of you stay where you are."

He was already accelerating as the Priest rolled over the side and into the back of the truck. In the mirror he could see several guns leveled in their direction.

"Zoe, hit the floor."

The truck's engine roared as it gave all it could, wheels grasping for purchase on the dusty road. A couple of shots rang out behind them but, thankfully, seemed not to hit anything important. Greg didn't ease off until the old roadhouse came into view, some five clicks later. He pulled into the parking lot, positioning them behind a stationary truck. It didn't look like anyone had bothered following them but better safe than sorry. Dim lights shone inside but all seemed quiet.

"Stay here, Zoe. I'll only be a minute."

The priest was curled up in the foetal position but sat up as Greg approached. His face was pale and streaked with soot and tears.

"Thank you. Thank you so much. You saved my life. I owe you…"

"You don't owe me anything, Padre. It was just the right time and the right place. You got lucky."

"Still…"

"What the hell was that all about anyway?"

"It was… unbelievable. I was leading prayers about the…"

The priest gestured towards the streaks in the sky.

"Yeah."

"That… and then Jimmy Jones started yelling. He was saying that God had abandoned them, that the Church had been lying to them all this time. It spread through the congregation like wildfire. I tried to calm them down but they were… they were a mob. They started shouting about burning the church down, like they hadn't been going for years… years and years. Jimmy Jones and Fred Campbell grabbed me. I… I don't know what they would have done if you hadn't shown up."

"I've got a fairly good idea. It doesn't take much to tip people over the edge. I'm not a religious man but I can see how they might think they've been abandoned."

The priest sniffed and shook his head.

"God moves in mysterious…"

"Yeah, I've heard that one. It doesn't help much when it comes down to the crunch though does it? Well, anyway, as much as I'd love to stand here philosophising, I've got somewhere I need to be. I'd be obliged if you'd hop out."

"What? You can't leave me here."

"Oh, I think you'll find I can. I intend to spend my last day, if that's what it turns out to be, with my daughter. I'm afraid you're not invited."

"What am I meant to do?"

"I don't know. Steal a car. Get drunk. I'm sure there's some booze in the roadhouse. Either way, that's your problem I'm afraid."

The priest clambered out of the flatbed and stood shivering in the night air.

"Well, thanks anyway. I owe you… and your daughter..."

Greg nodded and grinned.

"Like I said, you got lucky Padre. Let's hope it was worth it. Good luck."

The sun was creeping over the horizon by the time they

reached the top of the steep mountain road. Lines of purple and green blurred into the usual orange as night faded away. Zoe watched out of the back window, transfixed by the spectacular display in the sky. She hummed to herself, lost in her own private world. Her father's concentration was elsewhere. They'd soon be able to see the city that ran along the other side of the range.

His worst fears were realised as it came into view. Plumes of smoke and fire rose in both directions as far as the eye could see. Whole blocks had already been reduced to blackened remnants. Helicopters flew back and forth, some military, some emergency services. The similarity to scenes that he'd witnessed in his military days was obvious, but this felt entirely different. This was home. He had his daughter with him. He bit his lip, aware that he'd have to hold it together for both of their sakes.

"Daddy, why are all those places on fire?"

How could he explain this to her? What possible excuse could he come up with? The whole truth was more than she should have to bear at her age, but they had been through hell together and he had never lied to her.

"People are acting crazy because they're scared, honey."

"What are they scared of, Daddy?"

"They're scared of the strange light in the sky."

"Why?"

"Well… Some people are funny like that. They get scared of things they don't understand."

"Oh."

With all the natural nonchalance that only a six year old can muster, Zoe lost interest and turned back to staring out of the window. Greg exhaled, glad to be off the hook, and focused on the road ahead. They were descending now, getting ever closer to the chaos. A couple of cars roared past them heading the other way. He was glad it was them scraping the railings and not him. It was a long way down.

"Idiots."

By the time they reached the dual lane highway that ran in the shadow of the hills, it was daytime. The anomaly's black form loomed, looking like someone had cut a jagged hole from the sky. Greg gunned the pick up and headed east. They passed numerous wrecks, a couple of them still burning in the early morning heat. Traffic was light but the drivers were unpredictable, often not sober and meandering over the lines. He gave them a wide berth. The smell of combustion was strong now, combining with the omnipresent wail of sirens to strengthen the impression of being in a warzone. He eyed his shotgun, lying on the passenger seat, and hoped that he wouldn't have to use it.

"This is the turning for Mummy isn't it, Daddy?"

"Yes it is babe. Well remembered."

With relief he took the junction and followed the road as it meandered up past rows of identical white houses. A middle-aged woman in a smart trouser suit screeched something incomprehensible at them as they passed. She had a bottle of vodka in one hand and a bottle of rum in the other. Both were nearly empty. Greg turned back to his daughter.

"You alright darling?"

"Yes Daddy, I'm fine. I think that lady was drunk."

"I think you might be right."

The huge iron gates that led into the graveyard were wide open and Greg drove straight in. Normally he'd have gone up to the main building and parked there but he didn't want to be too far from the vehicle. He took a wide path only meant for pedestrians and hearses that took them straight up to their destination.

"Mummy!"

Zoe was already half way to the grave before he

could grab his gun and get out himself. He looked around nervously at the spattering of other mourners. They were all quite far away and more interested in their own dead than them. He relaxed and joined Zoe at his wife's burial place.

"Hey Mummy, hello! I hope you're sleeping well. The world has gone a little bit crazy and people are acting funny. I don't know if I like it, but it's all right. I'm not scared. Daddy's with me. Say hello Daddy."

"Hey honey."

They'd fallen into the habit of making conversation from their very first trip to her resting place. Somehow it had made the visits easier for them both. It had been four years since the disease had taken Selma and he doubted Zoe really remembered her anymore. This was the reality now. He watched as his daughter babbled away, telling her dead mother about the pictures she'd drawn, the television shows she'd watched… anything that came to mind. She seemed capable of almost endless chatter. She'd inherited that from Selma. He wasn't much for talking.

"Zoe, we'd better get going. Can you hop in the truck while I say a couple of words."

"OK Daddy. Bye Mummy. See you soon."

He watched her skip back to the truck, all golden hair and light. It made his heart heavy and he pushed back against the sensation. He turned back and knelt on the grass.

"Hey Selma. We're a little short on time but I wanted to tell you that we love you. I guess… well, it seems that the world might be about to end. I can't think of any other way of putting it. I'm hoping that it isn't true and all of this insanity is going to just go away, but chances are that it won't. So… this might be the last time we see you. Maybe we'll see you in another place. You know me, I'm not counting on it, but it sure would be nice. Anyway, rest easy. We need to go. See you on the other side."

He drove back through the suburb, aware that they were going to have to go through downtown to get to the beach. They crossed the highway. They passed smashed windows and closed shops, some of it clearly the aftermath of looting. Typical, Greg thought, that there were those whose first impulse in the face of impending doom was to grab a bigger TV. They started to see the occasional bloodied body in the street so he told his daughter to lie down in the back.

"I'll put the radio on so you can listen to some music. We should be there soon."

The news blasted out as soon as he flicked the switch.

"A mass suicide in a Chinese…"

He hit tune.

"Missiles launched into the heart of…"

This time he got lucky and the cab filled with the distorted sound of some classic rock band that he couldn't remember the name of. He knew Zoe was likely to complain but didn't feel inclined to keep looking.

"That's all there is today, honey."

A personnel carrier crammed with soldiers roared past them. They looked down at him, scoping them out. He forced himself to stare straight ahead, paranoid despite having nothing to hide. It seemed a strange way to spend your last day, if that's what it turned out to be… taking orders and running around on government business. The carrier swung left at the next intersection and disappeared. Greg breathed a sigh of relief.

The streets weren't as bad as he'd feared. Small groups of people stood around talking and drinking but there seemed to be little fight in them. He supposed that, judging by the state of the city, they'd had a heavy night. They were moving slowly now, negotiating burned out cars and other detritus that littered the streets. Nobody challenged them but that didn't stop him touching the shotgun once or twice for luck.

Finally they were clear and the coastal road lay ahead of them. The anomaly seemed even larger when seen looming over the open sea. The waters themselves were wild and tinged with purple and red. It seemed that others had had the same idea. Greg had wondered where all the children were, thinking that perhaps they were hidden away, sequestered from the abounding mayhem. Well, apparently a great many were here, playing obliviously under the watchful eye of their pale-faced parents.

"You can sit back up. It isn't far to go now."

Not wanting to join the masses he took them up beyond the city limits to where the coast began to curve back round on itself. There was a cove that he had used to visit with Selma back before Zoe was born, and with them both afterwards. It was small and could only be accessed by scrambling down a rocky incline. Mostly the general public kept away. The last time they had been was the day of the funeral. Something had kept him from wanting to return, although Zoe had asked a couple of times. Today though, it seemed as if he could think of nowhere else to go.

"Here we are. Come on honey, let's go to the beach."

There was an unusual electricity in the air that made the hair on the back of their necks bristle as they made their way down to the shore. The colours swirling around the anomaly were becoming more spectacular and Greg thought he could hear a faint buzzing that seemed to have no source.

"Can I paddle, Daddy?"

"Of course you can sweetie. Please don't go out too far. The waves are a little rough today."

"OK Daddy."

He sat down on the black sand and let the stress drain out of him. Here they were, the end of the road. Or was it? He still felt no fear; merely a little sadness that

Zoe might not get to grow old and take what pleasure there was to be had from living a life. Greg was an optimist though, didn't believe in fearing what the future might hold. Maybe they'd pass right through the thing and find some kind of existence in the beyond. He wasn't holding out for it, or if he was being really honest with himself, totally convinced that it was likely. It was possible though and for now that would have to do. Zoe was splashing and laughing in the cold sea, waving and smiling at him.

"Come on Daddy, the water's fine. Come on."

He smiled and waved back as he got back up. He kicked off his shoes.

"Watch out, here I come."

THE CARDIAC ORDEAL

"Daddy have some?"

"No honey, that's yours. You eat it up."

Shane forced a smile as Linda attempted to get another spoon into their daughter's mouth. The little girl wriggled and squirmed in her seat, always eager to find something more entertaining than eating. She would get round to it eventually but, at nearly two years old, saw no future in hurrying anything. A grubby hand reached out for her cup and swiped it onto the floor. Her laughter and delight subdued any anger her parents might have felt; she was just too cute to stay cross with.

"Do you want me to try and feed her?"

"You've got work. Don't worry about it. We've got all morning to eat breakfast."

Shane glanced at his watch and looked out of the window at the grey skies. It seemed like months since the weather had been anything approaching pleasant – probably an exaggeration, but he missed the summer months. At least then they could go and relax in the park on weekends. For the rest of the year they were virtual prisoners in their tiny home. They'd done their best to make it comfortable of course, but this aging council flat wasn't exactly bursting with potential.

"I need a holiday."

Immediately he regretted saying the words out loud. There was no mileage in complaining, and he couldn't face another argument.

Linda looked up from where she was sponging spilled milk from the ground. She looked tired, he thought. There were shadows under her eyes and her skin looked pale and dry. If anyone could do with a change of scenery, it was her.

"We need a holiday," he corrected.

"Maybe we'll be able to afford it next year." Her voice was a half whisper. "I should be able to work part time when Emma goes to nursery."

Living in the City did not come cheap. As well as the obvious things like rent, taxes and everyday bills, they both had student loans for degrees that somehow hadn't turned into lucrative jobs. At least we found each other he thought, scrabbling for a silver lining.

"Love you Daddy."

Then there was Emma. She was what kept them together and gave them the will to keep going. Throwing off the shadow of gloom that was enveloping him he reached across the table and grabbed her hands.

"I love you too pumpkin. To the moon and back…"

"Moon!" she shrieked and giggled, pulling her fingers free from his.

He pulled a face and swigged the remains of his coffee before standing up. His chair screeched as it dragged across the worn vinyl flooring.

"I'd better go."

"OK. Cheer up. How can you be sad when we have a little monkey like this in the house?"

"I'll be fine. I'm just tired."

"Say goodbye to Daddy, Emma. He has to go to work."

"Bye bye, Daddy, bye bye."

He leant over his daughter and kissed the top of her head, breathing in her scent as if it might sustain him through the day. She smelled of freshly baked biscuits and it lifted his heart.

Shane arrived at work out of breath and out of sorts, barely swiping his entry card in time to avoid losing an hour's pay. The gate clicked and he was inside. He dashed to the cloakroom, where several acquaintances were donning the long blue lab coats that the company insisted on.

"You look like you had to run, mate. Alarm not go off?"

"Somebody jumped in front of the train again."

"Poor bastard. I can sympathise."

"With me or him?"

"Ha, both I suppose."

"Well I'm alright, even if I did have to stand all the way. I expect they're still scraping him off the tracks."

"It might be my imagination but it seems to be happening more and more often these days."

"I think you're right. Hard times…"

"What a way to go though. I often wonder if they plan it in advance. My theory is that they're just standing there one morning, look around at all the miserable faces, and the urge just takes them. Screw it. Boom! They've traumatised some poor driver for life. Game over."

Before Shane had a chance to respond, a loud bell signalled the beginning of their shift. Like obedient Pavlovian dogs they padded out into the massive warehouse and went to work. It was repetitive and thankless labour; robots retrieved stock from the darkened recesses of the building and he then transferred it by hand to the packaging department. There was a supervisor but Shane had only spoken to her once or twice; he took his orders from a small scanning device that hung from his belt. It was a twilight existence, dimly lit and smelling of oil and plastic.

That morning was like any other. He walked back and forth until another bell announced that it was lunchtime. His work coat was barely back on its hook before his mobile phone started ringing. It was Linda.

"Shane? Shane… she's gone."

Once the police had finally left they found themselves sitting opposite each other at the kitchen table. It had been a madhouse when Shane got home, a maelstrom of questions and activity. Now that they were gone the silence was palpable and there were only the darkest of thoughts to fill that void.

Linda was clearly in shock, her tear-stained face pale and drawn. Shane could think of nothing to say that hadn't already been said, or that wouldn't make it seem as if he blamed her. Of course he couldn't help but do exactly that. He hadn't been here after all, and anyway, how could anyone lose a child in their own flat? How could Emma have disappeared in the brief moment that her mother had turned away? Had something unthinkable happened that she just couldn't admit?

"You blame me, don't you?"

"No, of course not."

They both looked at the empty high chair at the same time.

Shane lay in bed staring at the ceiling. He felt brittle, as if he might shatter into a thousand pieces at any moment. Where was she? His mind raced through the possibilities, never settling on anything. Linda lay beside him, unconscious thanks to the ministrations of a police doctor. She had been hysterical while they went about their business and the sleeping pills were an act of kindness. Now she lay on her back like a corpse, arms by her side.

He listened to the sounds of London, the faint buzz of traffic and distant sirens. It was the same background noise that he fell asleep to every night, but now he could imagine his daughter calling out for him, calling out for help. It was a vast jungle for someone so small to be lost in.

"Sod this."

Tired of torturing himself he got up and pulled on his clothes. His watch read midnight. Grabbing his coat he headed out of the front door with the intention of having a smoke and clearing his mind. The moment that the latch clicked behind him, one of the other two flats on the shared landing opened their door.

A face appeared. It was a middle-aged man, red-eyed and skeletal. His thinning grey hair seemed to be the remnants of a Mohican and his ears bore multiple piercings. He looked Shane up and down slowly and nodded.

"So, you lost your little girl?"

"I… She's gone missing, yes. I suppose the police spoke to you?"

"Me? No, I don't like talking to the police. I don't live here anyway. Christ, don't you even know who lives next door? What's the world coming to?"

"Well, we…"

"Calm down. I'm just yanking your chain. You're Shane, yeah?"

"That's right."

"Well Shane, I might be able to help you out. The only thing is that you have to do me a few favours first."

"What do you mean help me out? I don't understand."

"With your daughter I mean. You'd like to see her again wouldn't you?"

A wave of nausea passed over Shane.

"What do you mean? Do you know something? Where is she?"

Shane was suddenly in the man's face; ready to do whatever violence it took to get Emma back. The adrenaline headache was almost instant.

"Where is she? Tell me now before I do something I regret."

"Calm down mate, calm down. You need to take a deep breath. She's not here. I can help you but you have to do a few things for me first."

"What? Are you blackmailing me? I'll…"

"Chill. You're not going to like this, but you have to accept what I'm saying or you'll never see – what was it, Emma? – again."

"What if I go to the police? What then?"

"Then this conversation never happened and you've lost any chance of seeing your daughter alive again. You can't go to the police; you can't speak to your wife. If you do either one of those things, and trust me I have ways of knowing if you do, then I will just disappear. You could risk it of course, it's a free world, but I guarantee you that this is your one and only chance."

The man shrugged as if to say he didn't care either way.

"What do you think? Can you deal with that?"

"That's… This is insane. You have to tell me where my daughter is. Now."

"Last chance, Shane… Will you do what I ask or shall we just pretend this never happened?"

"Wait… I… What do you want me to do?"

"Now we're talking. Keep your head mate and this could end all right. The first thing that I want you to do is sort of a test, a starter for ten as they say. I want you to steal a book for me. It'll be easy. The owner is bedridden, a little old lady. You can just stroll in and pinch it. Wait there, I'll write down the title and address for you."

He kept his head down on the bus, horribly aware that there was bound to be a camera onboard. The leafy avenues of Primrose Hill were not his usual habitat, and just being here made him uncomfortable. Never mind that, he told himself; he had a job to do and that was all that mattered. Focus on the goal, think of Emma.

His hands were shaking when he got off at his stop. He stuffed them into his pockets and looked around. He was already on the right road so it was just a matter of finding number twenty-three. Odd numbers were on the other side, so he crossed over.

"Good morning."

Shane jumped. It was just an old man and a dog. He mumbled a greeting and walked on. Number twenty-three was much like the others. A low wall sat in front of a small garden that led up to a large creeper-covered Victorian terrace house. Not wanting to draw attention to himself he walked up the path and round to the left as he had been instructed.

There was a locked wooden door at the entrance to the back garden. Taking a deep breath he shimmied up and over it, landing with a thump on the other side. Instead of the neatly groomed plot that he'd anticipated, there was an overgrown mess. He could see various garden implements buried in the undergrowth and a small shed that had half collapsed at the back. Keep going, he whispered to himself.

Drawn curtains covered both of the back windows. He stepped up to the back door and tried the handle, fully prepared to smash his way in if it was locked, but the door opened at first try. Inside it smelled of cats and stale tobacco; it was oppressive and unwelcoming. He passed a kitchen on his left and a small bathroom on his right. The library was next and he stepped in.

The dim room only increased his sense of unease. He pictured getting caught in here. There was only one exit. Come on Shane, it's just a little old lady. Do it for Emma. Each wall had a bookcase, resplendent with cobwebs and dust. He peered at the titles, desperate to find what he was looking for. There was no kind of order and he was forced to look through them all. Half were foreign; some had nothing written on their threadbare spines. Eventually though he found it. As he reached out something slithered past his ankles. His chest tightened and he suppressed the urge to scream as he spun round to see a cat running from the room.

"Bloody hell. Nearly gave me a…"

The heavy footsteps on the stairs did not sound like they belonged to a frail old woman. Shane had no intention of waiting to find out. With the book under his arm he dashed out into the hallway and back into the garden.

"Come here you."

A quick glance over his shoulder revealed a bald behemoth striding towards him. Stuffing the book into his jacket he scrambled over the closed garden door and ran.

"Stop thief!"

Shane ran like he had never run before, ignoring the shooting pains cutting through his chest. His legs felt like limp spaghetti and he was concerned that they might just give out from under him. Fortunately they held and he managed to leave his pursuer behind.

Late afternoon shadows were winding their way across the pavement as Shane climbed the steps to his flat. He looked around furtively to see if anyone was watching; it would have been difficult to explain what he was doing to Linda and he wasn't sure that he would have much sympathy if he were caught by accident. His emotions were a strange mixture of doubt, fear, loss and the smallest amount of hope as he knocked. It was answered immediately.

"Ah, it's you. How did you do? Got it? Well done, well done. Right, that was the easy part. You'd better come in. Time for step two."

"I see. All right. Thank you. Yes, of course. Thank you. Bye."

Shane watched Linda hang up.

"No news. They want us to call them if we hear anything."

"Of course."

"They might do a press conference."

"Jesus."

They stared at their bowls of cereal without enthusiasm, lost in thought.

"I…"

They both spoke at once. Linda frowned.

"Sorry. You go ahead."

"No. It's fine. You first."

"I… I think I'll go and see Mary for a while today. Get out of the flat."

Shane sighed with relief.

"That's a good idea. I might go for a walk. Did me good yesterday."

"Right. Good."

"OK then."

Shane wondered how they could carry on from here, from this specific moment in time. Back to normality seemed such a long way up, he doubted either of them would have the will or strength to make that journey. Even if they got Emma back, their lives had been broken. He could see it in her eyes and he was sure that she could see it in his. Perhaps they would find something acceptable, a state of being that they could settle for, but he doubted it. After what he was going to have to do today, it seemed doubtful that he would even be able to live with himself.

He looked up from the table at Linda. She was watching him but turned away when he caught her eye. There was nothing positive they could say to each other.

"I think I'll go out now. I need some fresh air."

"Alright. I'll see you later."

"Right…"

He hesitated, still hoping to find something reassuring to say, but words failed him. Best he just do what he had to do –perhaps then they could connect again.

"See you later."

Once outside he allowed himself a breath of relief before processing the next nightmare that he had to deal with. The agony that he and Linda were feeling, the bottomless pit of loss that Emma's disappearance had engendered, and the price that he had to pay to try and fix all this; they were not things that he could deal with simultaneously. He was in danger of simply curling up into a ball and screaming if he couldn't find it within himself to compartmentalise these pressures.

His destination was within walking distance. He was glad of that. The bus had made him nervous and that was for a simple theft. This time anonymity was key. Of course this was London, and anonymity seemed ubiquitous, but that was a dangerous mindset for today. Perhaps he should have worn a disguise, but then Linda would have questioned what he was doing. He would just keep his head down and trust that luck was on his side. If he was caught later, so be it. As long as Emma was safe again it really didn't matter.

He arrived outside the office at two minutes before ten. The initial doubt, temporarily washed aside by desperation, had returned, threatening to derail him from his purpose. He leant against the wall and took some deep breaths, pictured his smiling daughter and reminded himself why he was here. It was difficult to reconcile the insanity of such an act with the purity of his purpose, or maybe trying to do so was in itself lunacy, but he had to be strong.

"Right…"

There were three names and three bells next to the tatty black door. The top one read 'Daniel Knight –

Solicitor'. He pressed it and the intercom crackled in response.

"Come on up. Third floor."

We've made an appointment for you at ten. Just go in. Do it and leave. It'll be over in no time.

This was it. He took the first and second flights of stairs quickly then paused on the third. He pulled the thing that they had given him from his pocket.

Make sure you give it a few seconds to warm up.

He switched it on, counted to five and carried on up the stairs.

Don't feel bad. He's a terrible person. Just think of your daughter.

"Come in."

Shane put the Taser behind his back and entered. Knight was sitting at a desk crowded with piles of books and paperwork. The walls were lined with old filing cabinets, some with their drawers half open. The man himself was red-faced and obese, sweating in a pinstripe shirt. He didn't wear a tie.

"Welcome, welcome. You're right on time. Now, let me see. Was this to do with a house purchase?"

Shane's fingers tightened around the weapon. The sound of his own heart beating almost drowned out the man's words. He had to do it now or he never would.

"I'm sorry…"

He stepped towards the desk and pointed the Taser at Knight's chest.

"What the hell is that?"

Knight rose from his seat, inadvertently making himself an easier target. Shane fired and two electrodes shot out and stuck to the astonished solicitor. Electricity arced across the wires and into his body.

He has a pacemaker.

The target froze, rigid for a moment, before falling forwards and knocking the contents of the table flying. His head hit the wood with a crunch and Shane could see blood as Knight slumped backwards onto the floor. He walked cautiously round to the body.

Double check that he's dead. Dead is the deal.

Daniel Knight was not coming back. His eyes were wide open and motionless, and there was pink drool on his lips. Shane flicked the off switch and pulled the wires free from the gun before stuffing it into a pocket. Time to leave. On the narrow stairs he met a silver-haired woman in a business suit coming the other way.

"I heard a bang. Is everything alright?"

Shane didn't answer, just pushed past her and ran down as fast as he could. Once he was out in the street he took off, turning into the first side street that he came to. Nobody appeared to be giving chase but he kept going until, winded, he had to stop and catch his breath. Nobody gave him a second glance, despite his guilt feeling like a neon sign above his head. There was a bus stop just along from him where half a dozen people stood milling about, as if it was just another day. How could they not know? How could it not be obvious that he had ceased to be like them, that he was now a killer?

As he walked the rest of the way back home he tried to fill himself with hope. Hope was all that he had now. The return of his daughter was the only thing that could compensate in any way for what he had done. Without it he was doubly destroyed. He tried to imagine what it would be like to hold her again, to lift her up and squeeze her tight, to see her smiling face. He couldn't hold on to the thought though. He kept thinking about what he had done. The path that he had taken might well secure her safety, but he would never be the same.

The door opened before he could knock and his nameless tormentor appeared. His face was twisted into a grotesque smile.

"Here he is, the man of the hour! Come inside, come inside."

Shane stepped into the hallway of the tiny flat and pulled the door closed behind him.

"Where is she?"

"Hold on now mate…"

"Don't give me that, where the hell is she…"

Shane grabbed a handful of the man's shirt, his self-control slipping away.

"Woah there, you need to be careful. You're only one step away from seeing the girl. One step…"

"Really? I'm starting to doubt she's even alive. I ought to…"

"Let me go and I'll prove it to you. Take a deep breath mate, before you hurt yourself."

Shane forced himself to step back.

A small lock of golden hair appeared in the man's hand.

"I thought you might ask, so here you go."

It vanished again, as quickly as it had appeared.

"That's not proof. How do I know it's hers?"

"It's hers. That's all you have to know. Now, the question that I have to ask you is this: how badly do you want her back? Is she that important to you?"

"I've just killed a man for you and you're asking me how important she is to me? Do you have kids?"

"God, no…"

"She means everything to me, everything. I'd do anything to get her back."

"Now we're talking. You might just get to see her again at this rate."

"Might? After what I've done?"

"You've got one more thing to do and then you'll have her back. I swear to you, on my Mother's grave, one more thing. This is what we've been building up to. You're not going to like it, but the choice is entirely yours. Do this one thing and you get to see little…"

"Emma."

"Emma, that's it. Do this one thing for me and you

get to see Emma again."

"Name it."

"Bring me your wife's heart."

"What?"

"Cut your wife's heart out and bring it to me. Then we're done."

"You're crazy. I'm not doing that."

"The choice is entirely yours mate. That's the price. You can rant and rave, as I'm sure you'd like to, but that's how it is."

"I can't…"

"Tell you what, have a think about it. Hopefully I'll see you back here shortly with what I want. If not, no hard feelings."

Linda was sitting at the kitchen table. Her eyes were red and puffy and damp streaks stained her cheeks. She watched him come in.

"I didn't expect you back so soon."

"No, I didn't think you would be here either."

Shane walked over to the kitchen sink and leant against it with both hands, his back to Linda. He closed his eyes. His body ached and he felt as if his spine might break from the invisible weight bearing down on him. How had he managed to get to this point? Without thinking he pulled open the drawer where they kept their carving knife.

"It's not in there."

He turned slowly. Linda stood behind him, the missing item gripped tightly in her hand. His gaze wavered from her face to the blade and back again.

"So he got to you too? Really? Why didn't you tell me?"

"Why didn't you tell me?"

"He told me not to. I didn't want to risk it."

"Same."

"Give me the knife."

"No."

"Put it down at least."

"No."

"So you're going to kill me then? Cut out my heart?"

"I don't want to but…"

"Emma."

"Shane, I have to get her back. I have to."

"There has to be another way Linda. I don't want to die."

"Sorry."

Her expression hardened and she lunged towards him. He grabbed her wrist before the point reached him and they struggled for control of the knife. He was larger and had weight on his side, but she was determined. Just when he thought he had loosened her grip, she bought her knee up and he had no choice but to back away momentarily.

"This is madness."

He grabbed a chair and held it out in front of him, swinging it as he advanced on her.

"You can't win, you know. Throw it away."

"Someone has to die."

The blade shook in Linda's grasp but she showed no sign of letting go.

"Look, we could go next door together. Force him to tell us where she is."

"Someone has to die… for Emma."

"No…"

She tore her own throat open with a vicious slash, cutting through to the artery and sending a spray of crimson arcing over him. He could only watch as the knife fell to the floor and she grasped at the wound, an expression of surprise fading while she bled out in front of him. She seemed to be trying to say something but he couldn't make it out. She made a last desperate gurgling sound and then she was gone.

Shane sunk to his knees and wept, devoid of thought

or understanding, drowning in darkness. When he could cry no more he steeled himself to do what had to be done. He butchered her in silence, mechanically, until he held her still-warm heart in his hands. He staggered to his feet and carried it outside.

Next door was unlocked and open, a crack of darkness clearly visible from outside. He elbowed his way into the flat.

"Here it is. I've got what you wanted. I've done what you asked. Give me my daughter."

His voice echoed around the empty rooms. There was nobody there, nor any sign that there ever had been. There was nothing.

MEAT SWEETS

Moses allowed himself a smile as he surveyed the room. Business was booming. There was an inexhaustible hunger for his 'specialist' meat products that he would never have imagined possible. Prices were through the roof and he had wasted no time in building a brand new barn. There was now room for twenty-five beds and they were all occupied. Of course it hadn't been easy. Since Gideon had died he had to shoulder all the hard work himself and fertile young women didn't simply grow on trees. He must have driven a good thousand miles in his quest for hitchhikers who fitted the bill. When he wasn't out hunting he was stoking up the furnace to dispose of unwanted males and when he wasn't doing that he had a million other things to consider.

After Marylyn caught him taking personal care of the spermatising, and had given him a solid beating, it became necessary to sit down and rethink that part of the process. At first he'd tried using a couple of drifters that he'd caught camping down in the bottom field, but quite frankly their performance had been disappointing. If he was honest with himself he found them a little distasteful and so he had gone the mechanical route. Moses wasn't an educated man but he had found himself enjoying the long evenings reading up on the fine art of insemination. The names of the drugs rolled off his tongue in a satisfying manner and he found himself repeating them as he went about his rounds. Sometimes he even sang them to himself.

'Cystorelin, Estrumate, Lutalyse. Cystorelin, Estrumate, Lutalyse.'

These were just the bovine medicines that his friendly veterinarian, a faithful customer, was happy to provide in quantity. From there he had moved onto clomiphene and gonadotropins. These substances were so sacred that they were actually meant for human consumption. The fat medical tomes that he laid out on the kitchen table were full of possibilities. Marylyn would bring him tidbits and sweet meats to chew on while he traced each line with his stubby fingers.

He kept all of these substances in a refrigerated cabinet that was his pride and joy. Always polished to perfection, it sat humming happily next to his collection of applicators and syringes. Marylyn had bought him one of those white coats that scientists wore and she was happy to keep it crisp and clean for him. Wearing it gave him an almost religious sense of purpose. He considered himself an 'expert', and when his wife jokingly called him Doctor Moses over breakfast one morning, it had put a smile on his face that lasted all day.

Now it simply wasn't enough for things to work as nature intended. That might have been sufficient for any other un-ambitious baby farmer but not for this man. No. There was a lot of scope for improvement. Gestation was a bottleneck that he was determined to defeat. Nine months was far too long to wait for every crop. It was time to experiment. He immersed himself in articles about fertility and childbirth. He read so much that, at night, he would dream that laughing fetuses were dancing around his bed crooning his praises.

His first attempts had been unfortunate. Several of

his best breeders had died at his hands, and there had been a fair amount of unpleasantness to deal with. Moses was an incredibly stubborn man though and he pushed on with his work. Although actual genetic modification was far beyond his remit, he still mixed his sperm samples together and doused them in chemical cocktails. This unprofessional approach had yielded few results, but now he was sure that his hard work was about to bear fruit. He could feel it in his water.

May had been with him the longest. He had a particular soft spot for her and so far had resisted meddling with her pregnancies. She'd churned out eight delicious little infants for him over the years and her milk was legendary. However this was precisely why he had taken the hard decision to get her involved. May was like a lucky charm and he needed all the good fortune he could get.

A faint clanging sound rose above the room's piped music bringing him back to reality. It was Marylyn ringing the breakfast bell. As he walked back to the house the smell of bacon reached him and his stomach rumbled in anticipation. He'd slaughtered one of the porkers the day before and he was eager to taste her. She had grown huge in captivity and he expected her to be some good eating. He'd spent a good half an hour selecting a fine blade for the slaughter and the actual act had naturally been a great pleasure. It was the circle of life or whatever it was that cartoon lion had called it. For a split second she had seemed to remember her former life as a legal secretary, but it had been fleeting. As he cut her throat she had been pure pig, squealing like the animal she was.

"Morning darlin'," he said as he sat down at the kitchen table.

"Darling," said his wife, blocking out the light as she loomed over him. "Someone's in a good mood today."

He stuffed a fork full of food into his mouth. A

stream of grease ran down his chin as he chewed happily.

"You know what? I am in a good mood. I think today's the day."

"Well ain't that nice."

Marylyn was very proud of Moses. Not only was he an excellent provider but also he had turned out to be such a clever man. In her mind's eye she liked to imagine him receiving a prize for what she imagined to be his groundbreaking research. That'd show all those know nothings who had made her childhood hell. She'd have loved to see all their stupid faces then.

"I was thinking we might keep the little 'un for ourselves this time. What's ten thousand dollars compared to some good eating? We're going to do ourselves some celebrating."

Overcome by emotion Marylyn leant in behind Moses and hugged him with arms like ham hocks. He patted her hand and then swatted her away.

"Come on honey, I'm eating here."

She smiled and disappeared out of the room. When she returned she was hiding something behind her back.

"Now I was saving this for Christmas but all things considered I don't think Jesus would mind if I gave it you early."

She held out a gleaming stethoscope.

"I think you'd look real nice wearing this."

Moses swallowed the last of his breakfast and threw down his cutlery. After wiping his mouth with his sleeve he turned and gazed up at her. There was a small tear in the corner of his left eye.

"Oh, you're such a sweet little thing."

He got to his feet and embraced her before planting a moist kiss on the top of her head. Releasing her he took the gift and put it round his neck.

"How do I look?"

"Like George Clooney on E.R."

He laughed and slapped his thigh.

"You're too much sometimes, honey. Right, this man has work to do. Wish me luck."

There was a spring in his step as he crossed the yard humming to himself. 'Cystorelin, Estrumate, Lutalyse. Cystorelin, Estrumate, Lutalyse.'

He unlocked the door and stepped inside. After slipping his lab coat over his checked shirt he straightened the stethoscope and rubbed his hands together. A muzak version of Ted Nugent's 'Weekend Warrior' was droning over the sound system. He felt good.

As he walked along the row of cubicles he inspected the other girls. He'd already done so earlier but he'd learnt that attention to detail hurt nobody. Many years ago one of his captives had escaped and he'd had a hell of a time tracking her down. Fortunately for him she'd fallen in a ditch and broken her ankle before she could get off his land. Of course he'd had no choice but to euthanize her there and then, but it had left a bad taste in his mouth. Now each girl was securely chained down and he was generous with sedation. Lesson learnt.

He peered in at his latest acquisition, a pretty girl by the name of Jackie. Miraculously she had already had a bun in the oven when he found her standing besides her broken down S.U.V. She had been looking a little green recently and he was concerned about her. She seemed to be doing all right now though. Her eyelids fluttered slightly as he got closer to listen to her breathing. It was shallow but regular.

May was snoring when he reached her. Her hands were resting on her swollen belly. She was only six months gone but she looked more than ready to pop. He walked over to his fridge and pulled out a small bottle marked 'Misoprostol'. Moses had been looking forward to using this. After reading an article in the 'New Scientist' he had moved heaven and earth to get hold of it. He unwrapped a fresh syringe and pierced the lid. Once it was loaded with double the recommended dose he returned to May.

"Here we go."

The substance took effect immediately. May's chains clattered as she started to shake and she emitted a guttural howl. Moses frowned. According to the books it should have taken some time to work.

"Come on now, Daddy's here. Ain't nothing to worry about."

A ripple of activity crossed over her belly. Something was moving beneath the surface. She gripped the side of her bed and howled again. He bit his lip and watched as she instinctively pushed in parallel with the muscle spasms that the drug was inducing.

"Good girl. Keep it coming."

Moses took a glimpse 'down under' as Marylyn liked to say. Apart from an ominous twitching there was no sign of the child. He ran his tongue over his teeth, not quite sure what to do next. Waiting was not one of his strengths. Realizing that he had forgotten to wear sterile gloves he walked off to retrieve a pair. Once he'd pulled them on he returned to May.

At first he missed the tiny fingers gripping the sides of her most intimate parts. When he saw them he did a double take. It made no sense. As he puzzled over this her lower lips were suddenly torn asunder. May's body shook in violent spasm for a few seconds and then fell still. Flesh ripped and a gaping wound was created between her thighs. From this newly expanded orifice a head appeared. In essence it was that of a baby, at least it was roughly the correct shape, but Moses' knees buckled at the sight of it. The skin was rough and blackened as if burnt. The eyes, yellow and feral, stared at him with an intensity that put the fear of God into him. It was without lips so that its jagged teeth were permanently on display. When it saw the farmer staring at him the mouth opened and a bowel splitting screech filled the air.

Moses instinctively looked around for a weapon but there was none. He watched in horror as the child pulled itself free from its mother's body. A wave of putrid black liquid gushed onto the bed. The smell was hideous and he gagged as the stink washed over him. Around the room the other inhabitants began to groan and writhe and rattle their chains.

The ugly baby crouched on all fours and leapt at Moses. As it struck his chest it bounced back, restricted by the still attached umbilical cord. It hit the edge of the bed and fell onto the floor. The cord was still holding firm but after a few tugs it came free bringing the placenta with it. The child skittered across the cold concrete and disappeared under a bed. A dark trail was smeared across the floor where it had been.

Moses looked down. As he did so his stethoscope fell apart and the pieces rained down onto his feet. His coat was smeared with filth. He looked at the eviscerated remains of May and slowly shook his head.

"You're going to regret this little man. It. Is. On."

It took him about thirty seconds to run out and retrieve his shotgun and a pocketful of cartridges from the cab of his pickup. When he returned the wailing and screaming had intensified but it didn't seem like the child, or thing, had moved.

"Come out of there."

Nothing. Cautiously he edged over and pushed the bed aside. The child rushed off, trailing its glutinous package behind it. Moses got off a shot. The placenta exploded but the baby was unharmed. It veered towards Jackie's bed. Moses swung the gun round and fired again. This time the shot went wild putting a large hole in the girl's side.

"Hell fire."

The child kept moving and Moses reloaded. His next attempt shattered the glass on the front of his beloved drugs cooler.

"You're going to pay for that in spades, boy."

More shots rang out and more carnage ensued. Two more girls were given a bloody release from their ongoing torment. One poor innocent lost her head and the little thing leapt onto the bed and basked in the arterial fountain. It stuck its tongue out and lapped up the salty plasma as it fell.

Moses saw red and charged, his shotgun now reversed and held out like a club. He swung it but before it could connect he lost his footing on the slippery floor. There was a crack as his head hit the concrete floor. Darkness swamped his consciousness and he blacked out.

When he came round he wasn't sure how long it had been. The little one was gone. A trail led to the door. It didn't go straight there though. Looking around he could see that while he was asleep the thing had been to every bed in the room. His skull throbbed as he went from girl to girl. Their throats had all been torn out.

With a wail of frustration and fury he hobbled out of the new barn and crossed the yard over to the old one. This was where he kept his sharp items. A wall of gleaming pain potential greeted him as he entered. He selected a large machete and an orbitoclast. The latter was essentially a surgical ice pick intended for use in lobotomies. Marylyn had given it to him for his birthday. It had come in a beautiful presentation box.

Back in the yard he could see a bloody trail leading to the house.

"If you've done anything to that woman…"

Gripping his weapons he cautiously approached the front porch. His heart hammered at his rib cage as he imagined the damage he was going to do to that little bastard. Inside old Uncle Vern stared down at him from the cracked portrait that dominated the hallway.

"What the hell you doing boy?" it seemed to shout.

"Shut up. I'm getting payback," whispered Moses as he deftly avoided the floorboards that creaked the most.

Marylyn wasn't in the kitchen. That made him nervous. She was always in there cooking something up or bolting something down. The dead porker's head lay on a baking dish on the table surrounded by onions and peppers. Its hair had been shaved off and there were small cuts in the cheek where chopped garlic had been inserted. Its sightless eyes stared up at the ceiling. Marylyn had been making Cabeza, one of his favorite dishes. Damn, how he loved that woman.

A soft cooing from the front room caught his attention. He readied himself for action and followed the sound. The curtains were still drawn and it took his eyes a couple of seconds to adjust to the darkness.

"Marylyn?"

When his wife turned to face him he saw that the top half of her dress was torn away leaving her bosom exposed. Her eyes were wide and she had a half smile on her face.

"Moses?"

A shiver colder than a penguin's pecker ran down his spine as he realized that the baby was attached to her. It was feeding. That made no sense though. Marylyn's milk had run dry decades ago.

"What…"

There was a wet sound as the child detached itself and turned its head towards him. It hissed and bared its blood stained teeth before turning back to bury itself in her flesh once more. Marylyn's eyelids fluttered as she spoke her last words.

"Ain't he just the sweetest thing?"

SCORCH

"Sorry, we just don't have any more beds."

"We spent all day getting this money you know? We're soaked and bloody freezing… can't you just squeeze us in?"

"I really am sorry, but once the beds are full, that's it."

Toby put his hand on Lisa's shoulder.

"Come on. Let's go."

He felt her twitch as she considered tearing away from his grip. The pale individual behind the counter shrugged at him and shook his head.

"There's really nothing I can do."

It was obvious that Lisa was fighting back tears, more of anger than sorrow. He couldn't really blame her. Today had been hard, noticeably worse than those that had come before. Their reserves of pride and enthusiasm were almost gone, drained from them by just a fortnight on the street. Only the thought of sleeping in an actual bed had kept them going and now that hope was gone, it was hard to see how they could carry on.

"Come on."

Outside it was deserted. It was not the kind of evening that anyone would choose to spend outdoors unless forced to. The workers had returned to their nests and the tourists were sheltering in their hotels. It was bloody cold. Toby and Lisa staggered into the wind, instinctively eager to put some distance between them and the scene of their disappointment. Eventually they found themselves back by the canal, under the graffiti clad bridge where they had spent the last two nights huddled together for warmth.

"I don't think I can do this anymore."

Toby sighed. Truth be told he was terrified that she might just decide to leave him and go home to her mum. She could probably get away with it but there was no warm welcome waiting for him. If his father didn't batter him to death then hers would, and that was without considering the small matter of the stolen car that had got them here. No. It wasn't an option.

"Come on. We'll work something out."

"Like what?"

Christ she was beautiful, even now, even with despair written all over her perfect face. The thought of losing her was unacceptable. Two weeks in the big city had given her a grey pallor and she looked thin and tired. Her voice had taken on a weary edge, worn down by the constant to push back the encroaching darkness. Still, he couldn't imagine loving her any more than he did. She deserved everything he could give and more.

Toby was aware how fragile these things were, how little it would take for that connection between them to break, leaving him alone and heart broken. Not having a solution to their problems, struggling to rise to the occasion was killing him. He took a deep breath and pulled himself together.

"I don't…"

He stopped short, suddenly aware that she wasn't looking at him anymore, and turned around.

"Horrible night isn't it?"

The stranger smiled but there was no warmth to it. He was in his thirties, wrapped up tight in a long coat that looked like it had been expensive, a tweed flat cap pulled down low over his eyes. He seemed somehow inhuman, lizard like.

"It's no night to be out. Don't you two have homes to go to?"

His London accent echoed under the brickwork. Lisa and Toby stared at him but said nothing, still startled by his sudden presence and too inexperienced to know how to laugh off this banal attempt at engaging them in conversation. He looked at them with a hunger in his eyes.

"I have a house that's not too far from here. Nice and warm and dry. Maybe we could come to some kind of arrangement."

Toby's eyes narrowed and he felt his fists clenching of their own accord.

"Well, I live all alone and your girlfriend…"

"I can speak for myself you know. Talk to me."

"Of course, sorry. You are a very attractive girl you know."

"And…"

"And I'm wondering if perhaps you might be interested in…"

"What?"

"I do you a favour and you do me one. It could be fun. If you prefer, I could just watch. I've got some wine…"

Lisa's boot moved swiftly towards the man's crotch. He doubled up as it struck home, a strange sound coming from his lips. Then she was next to him, shoving him hard with both hands. He fell, landing sideways in the canal with a loud splash.

"Come on. Run."

She grabbed Toby's hand and pulled him along, his legs getting the idea just in time to avoid tripping over himself. By the time that the vociferous curses emanating from the water had faded and they were back amongst the houses they were both laughing.

"That was amazing."

"He deserved it."

"Slow down a minute."

Toby let go of her hand and stopped running, his breath heavy from the exertion. She came to a halt and stood grinning at him, her face lit up with amusement.

"Come on. We ought to get moving. He might call the police."

"Somehow I don't think he's going to call the police."

"Well, just to be on the safe side…"

They took a turn into a dimly lit side street, walking now at a steady pace.

"You know that now we've got to find somewhere new to sleep?"

"I didn't like it there anyway."

"Me either but we can't wander around all night, plus I think it's going to rain."

Toby looked up at the black clouds gathering in the starless skies overhead and shivered.

"We'll find something."

They both noticed the red brick house at the end of the street at the same time. It stood slightly apart from the others, alone, brooding, and clearly abandoned for some while. The front yard had only a few clumps of living grass in it, most of it asphyxiated by the piles of rubbish that passersby had thrown over the low wall. The windows had been bricked up and boards had been nailed over the front door. A dead shopping cart lay wheels up, doubtless dreaming of its glory days.

There was something that seemed somehow fortuitous about their discovery of this place. They both felt it. It called to them in their hour of need. They turned around and looked at each other but nothing needed to be said. This wasn't the first derelict house that they'd seen, far from it. London was full of them.

The difference was that up until now they'd always said that they wouldn't break in anywhere, that they weren't that desperate. Whether they had reached the end of the line or simply felt that they had reached the right place for them wasn't part of their thought process. All they knew was that if there was shelter here, then they were going to take it.

"Come on, let's see if there's a back door."

Lisa was first through the rusted ironwork gate. The house backed onto a tall concrete wall that was covered in graffiti. The front door had been bricked up but there was a back door with one plank barely hanging on to deter trespassers. She tugged at it lightly and it fell to the floor. She turned to Toby with a grin, he raised an eyebrow and shrugged, and without any further ado they went in.

"Will you look at this place? It's like something out of a history book."

There were none of the modern implements usually found in a modern kitchen. A dust covered standalone sink stood next to a simple wooden table covered with a rotting tartan tablecloth. A small gas cooker lurked in the corner of the room, several mouldy pans still in place.

"I don't reckon anyone has lived here for a while."

"You think?"

"What's that smell?"

"Smells like someone's burned something."

"Come on, let's explore."

The kitchen led out into a narrow hallway with the front door ahead of them. Shadows cast a patchwork of lines across a fading rug.

"It's a bit dim in here."

"Try the lights."

"They're not going to work."

"Try them anyway."

Toby found the switch and flicked it. Miraculously a lone bulb came to life.

"What if anyone sees us?"

"The windows are bricked up. I don't think anyone could. Anyway, I'm beyond caring to be honest. A nice warm jail cell sounds quite nice."

"Don't even joke about it."

"Who's joking?"

The sitting room had the same carboniferous odour as the kitchen, along with a hint of fungus. Its furnishings were sparse, consisting of only a couple of armchairs, a bookshelf and a precarious table with an old radio sitting on it. A thick layer of dust covered everything.

"My Nan used to have one of these. It didn't work though."

Lisa walked over and turned some dials. One clicked and a burst of static filled the room. She twiddled some more but couldn't tune into anything other than noise.

"Give it up. Come on, let's go and see what's upstairs."

"Sure. I'm exhausted."

Narrow stairs led up to a landing with just two doors. The first had no bulb in the light fitting but it was obviously a child's room. A crib, empty except for a tatty bear, stood up against the far wall. There was a mobile with cobweb encrusted angels hanging from the ceiling and an old chest of drawers, but otherwise it was empty.

"Creepy."

"Yeah, they didn't have much stuff in those days, did they?"

"It's not that though. Why is this still here? It doesn't look like anybody has lived here for decades."

"I don't know. Maybe some family owns it and just never got round to selling it. Maybe there's something wrong with the place."

"Asbestos."

"Bloody hell, maybe we shouldn't stay here then."

"Nah, it'll be alright. My Dad said that as long as you

didn't mess around with it, asbestos was all right. It's only when you start poking about at it that you get into trouble."

Toby cringed at the mention of her father.

"Right. No poking about then."

He turned and crossed over into the room opposite. Two single beds filled most of the room. A small dressing table and a corner wardrobe squeezed into the remaining space.

"Well it's not very romantic but the beds are made."

"Probably full of bed bugs. I think I'll use my sleeping bag."

"Me too."

They untied their bags from their packs and laid them out. Once they'd removed their boots and coats they clambered in, luxuriating in the comparative comfort.

"Oh man, this feels good."

"How the other half lives, eh?"

"Thanks babe."

"What for?"

"Letting us come in here. I know you didn't want to squat."

"No, I really didn't. I just don't want any hassle with the police, you know? There was something about this place though. It just felt like the right thing to do, like it was waiting here for us just when we needed it."

"That's what I thought. That and I'd had enough of being bloody wet."

They both laughed.

"Lisa."

"Yeah."

"I love you, you know. I'm sorry this is all so hard."

"Don't worry about it. I never thought it was going to be easy."

"And?"

"What?"

"The love bit..."

"Oh, sorry babe. I love you too. Now let's get some sleep."

They were both so fatigued that they fell asleep within minutes.

Some time later Toby woke with a start. He'd been having a nightmare in which he was on fire. He'd been running from person to person, screaming at them to help, to extinguish the flames. They'd regarded him with puzzled glances before carrying on with whatever trivial tasks they had been engaged with before. It had got hotter and hotter until finally he could feel himself turning to ashes. As the last vestiges of his body crumbled away, he'd come round coated in sweat.

Lisa was still fast asleep. Toby looked at his watch. One am. Feeling thirsty he squeezed out of his sleeping bag and headed downstairs to see if any of the taps were working. As he came to the sitting room door he heard music. It was the radio playing what he thought of as old people's music. Jazz or something.

"We'll meet again, don't know where, don't know when..."

He slumped down into an armchair and let the melody wash over him, the search for a drink completely forgotten. It felt unusually warm, considering the lack of central heating, and he was quickly asleep again, even before he noticed the way that the shadows in the room seemed to be creeping towards him.

Upstairs Lisa sat upright, suddenly awake. She was vaguely aware that she too had been dreaming but the details slithered away before she could grasp them.

"Toby?"

She looked across at his empty sleeping bag and called a little louder.

"Toby? Where are you?"

Still nothing.

"Weird."

She was still debating whether to leave her cozy sleeping spot to go and search for him when the crying started. It was a high-pitched wail that cut through her, triggering a maternal response that she would never have thought herself capable of.

"A baby?"

Disbelieving, she shrugged herself free of the bag and headed downstairs. It seemed colder than it had before, her breath forming crystal clouds in front of her. Surely there were more cobwebs than there had been before? The ceiling and corners were thick with them. As she entered the sitting room the lightbulb flickered and crackled, swinging slightly although there was no visible reason for it to do so.

"How did that get down here?"

It was the crib from the nursery. More of a basket on legs than anything else, it stood in the center of the room. The crying continued as she forced herself to look inside, convinced for some reason she couldn't fathom, that whatever lay within was best left untouched. Somewhere within her a battle raged between the need to intervene and the need to run. Curiosity elbowed her indecision aside.

"It's just a baby. Hello little one, what are you doing here?"

Lisa looked down at its little round face, aware that her heart was beating nineteen to the dozen. The child stared back up at her with blue eyes that seemed immediately familiar. Then it smiled, a lopsided smirk that belonged to someone much older, a grin that she had seen a thousand times before.

"Toby?"

Before she knew what she was doing, she had picked the baby up and was holding it to her, careful to cradle its head as her sister had taught her. It stopped crying and made happy snuffling sounds instead.

"What are you doing with my bloody baby?"

Lisa nearly dropped the baby in shock. The woman at her side had appeared from nowhere. Her face was horribly scarred down one side, the flesh misshapen and livid as if it had been exposed to an open flame.

"I said, what are you doing with my bloody baby?"

She had a thick cockney accent, but her voice was strangely thin, possessed of a slightly metallic overtone that left a ringing in Lisa's ears.

"I…"

"Give 'im 'ere, before I do something I blooming regret."

"But it's…"

"Now!"

Lisa ran from the room and into the dusty kitchen. She grabbed the handle on the back door but it was frozen in place. Clutching little Toby tightly, she ran back into the corridor and up the stairs.

"Come back 'ere…"

She didn't see the man on the landing until it was too late to stop herself from barreling into him. She twisted to avoid hitting him face first, or worse, with the baby. Then something strange happened. Rather than knocking him flat or rebounding off him, time seemed to slow down to a crawl, and she passed straight through him, coming to a stop on the other side. She turned to face him, aware that reality was once again running at a normal pace.

"How did…"

He held up his palms towards her arms outstretched. They were a wretched tangle of blackened meat and bone, the fingers twisted and broken.

"I tried, you know."

She looked up from his wretched hands and instantly regretted it. His eyes were the darkest thing that she'd ever seen. They made her feel lightheaded and nauseous. Her voice, when she spoke, seemed to come from far away.

"What did you try? I don't understand."

"To save him."

"From what?"

He tilted his head to the side, encouraging her to listen.

"Do you hear that?"

Lisa hadn't noticed before but there was now a different kind of wailing in the distance. It rose and fell, inhuman and foreboding. She tried to think where she had heard it before and clutched the baby closer to her.

"I don't… Is it an air raid siren?"

He didn't answer but simply looked up.

A low rumble filled the air, all pervasive enough that she could feel it rising up through the bones in her feet. Soon her entire body shook. She barely had time to consider how odd this felt, or why there was a sudden whistling in her ears, before everything turned to noise and fire. She watched in horror, orange and yellow flames billowing languorously towards her and the baby, engulfing them in a blistering heat. It grew brighter and brighter, hotter and hotter, until it could not possibly get any more intense. Then there was nowhere to go except darkness.

She was woken by something sharp prodding her in the side. Opening her eyes, she looked up to see an elderly lady wielding an umbrella.

"Ah, you're alive then. You don't want to be sleeping here dear, you never know what might live in all of this nasty rubble."

Lisa blinked and looked around at the bricks and dirt that she had been sleeping on. It made no sense.

"There was a bomb…"

"Yes dear. I was just a little girl then. I grew up just around the corner. Very sad, I remember they had a…"

"Baby?"

"That's right. Anyway, I must be going. Find yourself

a nicer place to sleep if you can, a lovely young girl like you. It's not right."

"Have you seen my boyfriend? He's called Toby…"

"No. Just you. I was on my way home. Good luck finding him. Bye now."

Lisa got to her feet and watched her go.

"Toby? Where are you? Toby!"

THE TEPPENYAKI OF TRUTH

Turner frowned. They had been travelling for more than three hours. A succession of deadbeat towns had flashed by, before being replaced by seemingly endless winding country roads. Now they were passing through a skeletal forest and the light was starting to fade.

"Hey buddy, how much further now?"

Unsurprisingly, the corpulent Japanese driver had not learnt to speak English since the last time that he had been asked the same question. He just smiled into the mirror and shook his head. Turner sighed and slumped back into his seat. It was a cliché, but he really was getting too old for this shit. Unfortunately money talked and he couldn't afford not to listen.

Every time a pay day came, he found himself in Vegas, blowing it all on the roulette wheel that never paid, the whores with contempt written all over their faces, and the coke that left him burnt out and hating himself. So it was that when a mysterious voice on the phone said it had a proposition for him, he had bitten so hard that it made his jaw ache. Now he was somewhere in the ass end of nowhere, Iowa, feeling his age and wishing he was somewhere else.

The car slowed and came to a halt outside a weather-beaten old diner. A lone neon Budweiser sign flickered in one of the filthy windows. His chauffeur squeezed himself out from behind the wheel and opened the door for him. Turner stepped out into the damp evening and shivered. An odour of decaying wood hung in the air.

"Thanks Buddy. I'd give you a tip, but I'm a little strapped at the moment."

The driver shrugged and climbed back into the car. He sped off leaving Turner standing alone in the moonlight.

"Right, let's do this thing."

The diner door was rotten and splintered. It screeched in protest as he pushed it open. He stepped inside. Before he had a chance to fully appreciate the graveyard ambience, a beautiful girl in a long red dress stepped out from the shadows. Her hair reminded him of Marilyn Munroe and she smelled of violets. Her presence in these surroundings was surreal.

"Mister Turner? Welcome. Mister Koboyashi will be with you in a few moments. My name is Mandy. Can I get you a drink? We have beer and whisky."

"A whisky would be fine, thanks babe."

He wished he was thirty years younger. Once upon a time, a girl like this might have fallen for his gangster talk and lean features.

Mandy went behind the counter, which had collapsed at one end, and poured him a large tumbler of Scotch.

"I'm afraid we have no ice."

"Straight up is good. Don't worry about it."

He took a big swallow of the golden liquid and slapped his thigh as it burned its way down his throat.

"Hey, that's pretty goo…"

The world unexpectedly folded in on itself and he fell down a deep black chasm into unconsciousness.

When he came around, he was in a different room. An aroma of oil and carbon hung in the air, and streaks of the same stained the walls. When he tried to move his head, it didn't respond. He tried lifting his arms but again nothing happened. He could sense straps around his wrists, legs and waist. The leather chair to which he was attached felt cold on his bare skin. Someone must have removed his clothes, but he couldn't tilt his head to be absolutely sure.

In front of him there was a large square hot plate, some four feet across and three feet deep. On either side of it were raised shelves. To the right was a row of bowls. He couldn't see what they contained. On the left a wide range of steel implements had been laid out. There were kitchen knives of various sizes, several spatulas, a small axe, and a variety of skewers. They gleamed as if they had recently been lovingly cleaned.

Once again, he struggled to move his scrawny body, but it was no use. He was paralysed. Even attempting to shout, and he had some choice words that he dearly wanted to release, had no effect. He stopped trying and allowed himself to listen. There was nothing to hear except the shallow wheeze of his own breathing. Despite the chill in the air he could feel individual drops of sweat as they rolled down his face. His muscles locked against each other as they attempted to shiver but were stopped by whatever was holding him still. He heard a door open and close behind him.

"Good morning, Mister Turner. My name is Hiro Koboyashi. Welcome to the Teppanyaki of Truth."

As the speaker walked into view, he was revealed to be a tall Japanese man, resplendent in a crisp white Chef's outfit topped with a magnificent toque. He had a broad face and a prominent nose. One side of his mouth was slightly higher than the other, giving him a permanent look of mild amusement. His voice was deep and assured, with only the mildest trace of an accent.

"So, Mister Turner, have you ever been to a teppanyaki restaurant before?"

After a brief nod in Turner's direction, he leant down

and adjusted some hidden controls. Then he picked up one of the bowls and poured a thin layer of oil over the warming surface. Taking a spatula in each hand he scraped it back and forth until it formed an even covering. The sound of metal on metal filled the room. Turner's eyes bulged as he watched.

"We cook and prepare your food in front of you. A good teppanyaki chef tells a story while he works. I suppose you could say that it's a kind of theatre."

Koboyashi set aside the spatulas and picked up a paring knife. He took a peeled onion from one of the bowls, rolled it onto the hot plate, and proceeded to chop it into tiny pieces. The blade moved with incredible speed, decimating the innocent vegetable. Once satisfied he twirled the knife high into the air, bowed, and caught it on the way back down.

"No doubt you are wondering why you cannot move or speak. We injected you with a substance that affects your nervous system. It makes things so much easier for me. I am sure that you have things that you would like to tell me, details that you might think will make a difference to what happens today, but rest assured, there is nothing that you can tell me that I don't already know."

He took a handful of rice and threw it on top of the diced onion. Picking up the spatulas again he used them to craft a sloping crescent from the pile. Happy with his efforts, he spun the spatulas in his hands for a moment, before putting them aside. Taking another bowl, he poured the dark liquid along the edge of the mound.

"Do you like my beach? Perhaps it reminds you of somewhere? No? I suppose a man like you has been to many beaches over the years. Let me help you with your memory."

Quick as a flash he grabbed the largest knife in his collection, leant over the hotplate, and grasped Turner's wrist. The chair titled forwards and Turner felt a burning sensation as his hand was pulled down onto the metal.

"Perhaps you remember one…"

The knife shone as it came down, removing a segment of his index finger. Pain shot up Turner's arm, but he couldn't pull away.

"Two…"

The end of his middle finger was severed.

"Three…"

Ring finger.

"Four…"

His little finger was suddenly no more than a ragged stump.

Koboyashi pressed the bleeding ends of Turner's digits onto the hotplate. After letting them sizzle for a few seconds he pushed Turner back upright.

"Yes. Perhaps you remember four little girls."

He pushed the fingertips up against the rice and onion dune with the edge of his knife.

"Four little girls playing on the beach."

Small streams of red mixed with the oil.

Sweat poured down Turner's face. Here and there a muscle twitched slightly under the surface as his whole body fought to move. The pain was unbelievable. He wanted to scream, to deny everything, but he could only watch and suffer. The truth hurt.

Steel scraped on steel again as Koboyashi tidied his creation. His face was still calm as he worked.

"Of course, you really should remember, because I know you were there. You went there in a…"

The knife dropped from his hand with a clang and was replaced by the axe. He leant forwards again and grabbed Turner's uninjured hand. Slamming it on to the hotplate, he bought the axe hurtling down. Tendons and muscles split as it embedded itself into the wrist. The hotplate sizzled once more as blood flowed over the scorching metal. Again, the blade came down. This time the radius and ulna shattered. A third blow was enough to separate it from the arm. Swiftly Koboyashi grasped the spurting limb and cauterized it. He then pushed Turner away again and, using the edge of the axe's blade, flipped the detached hand so it was palm up in the hot oil.

"You were there in a boat, weren't you? Such a pretty boat that the little girls couldn't resist when you offered them a ride. Or did you tell them a lovely story to get them to come aboard?"

Turner shook in his chair, and a low groan forced itself up from his gut. It was pain, not regret, and Koboyashi looked at him doubtfully.

"Really? You still don't accept the truth of what you did? Ah, Mister Turner, I know a liar when I see one, and I'm looking at one now. I am not fond of liars, but perhaps you have worked that out for yourself by now. It's time to turn up the heat, as you say."

He twisted a dial. The fingers on the inverted hand were twitching now, slowly contracting into a claw. Before they could close completely Koboyashi used a spatula to flick the fingertips one by one into the darkening palm. He scraped the beach that he had made into a hole in the plate, and tipped more oil around the hand.

"So, away you went with four little innocents in your grasp. Yet you only needed one, didn't you? I wonder how you chose. How does one choose such a thing?"

A faraway look crossed his face as he stood juggling the spatulas. Turner regarded his nemesis through a haze of agony and anger. He had received plenty of beatings in his time, but this level of pain was something altogether new. He yearned to black out but it seemed that he would receive no such mercy.

Koboyashi selected an unused knife with a serrated blade from his collection. He stepped around the teppanyaki table and disappeared from Turner's view. Turner willed his head to turn but couldn't manage it.

He felt a hand under his chin, pulling him back so that his neck rested against the chair. The next thing he felt was cold metal touching his ear lobe. It began to move back and forth in a sawing motion. Fresh waves of agony flowed over him. There was a strange ripping sensation as the knife cut the ear free.

"I thought that you might have allowed them to argue for their lives, that you may have listened to them begging to be spared. Then I realised that you are not the kind of man who listens."

The ear sailed over his shoulder and landed in the oil. It burst into flames and shrivelled up until it was no more than a blackened lump of carbon.

"No, Mister Turner. You are not a man who cares what others have to say. I think it's fair to say that you are not a man who cares about others at all. So, how would you make such a decision?"

The grip on his chin relaxed for a moment, as Koboyashi stretched round to find a skewer. Once he had it, the grip tightened again. Turner felt a small cut being made in the flesh around his eye and then something being forced into the socket. It was the rounded end of the skewer. With a wet pop, his eyeball was released onto his cheek. For a moment the world swung back and forth before coming to a rest, leaving him with an awkward view of his own naked body. It was pale and splashed with specks of red.

"I think that you are the kind of man who makes decisions based on your own shallow observations. You have little time for thought beyond your own pleasures. I think you made your choice simply from the way these little girls looked to you."

Without warning, Turner's head was pushed forwards so that his eyeball dangled in mid-air. He could see the hotplate getting closer and closer. The heat was intense. As it touched the metal, cornea and iris evaporated and the vitreous fluid bubbled and frothed.

Crazed flashes of blinding light ricocheted down his optic nerve. Koboyashi pulled him back into the chair again and the pulped remains of Turner's eye splashed onto his face. It burnt.

The chef reappeared in front of him. Turner's one-eyed vision was blurred, adding to his diminishing sense of reality. Koboyashi had picked up a pair of saltcellars and was throwing them from hand to hand. He threw one up and bounced it off his elbow so that it landed on the top of his hat. Leaving it there, he sprinkled a layer of crystals into the oil.

"So, you threw three into the sea."

He took a spatula and tapped three of the fingertips out of the hand and onto the plate. They burst into flames and he pushed them down into the rubbish chute.

"This just left the two of you. Nasty Mister Turner and poor little Stacey. Am I getting the story right?"

Turner shuddered. Koboyashi smiled.

"I think it's time that you were given a chance to speak for yourself. Mandy!"

The hidden door swung open. Turner couldn't see her, but recognised the waitress's perfume. There was the rattling of a tin being opened and then a new pain in the side of his face.

"Just enough antidote so that you can move your mouth, Mister Turner. I hope that you are ready to give us the truth."

The needle was removed.

"Thank you, Mandy. You may leave us now."

Koboyashi looked down at the blackening hand. The meat was crumbling away, leaving a nest of bones grasping the scorched remains of Turner's ring finger. A grey plume of smoke wound its way up to the ceiling.

"So, Mister Turner… are you ready to tell the truth now?"

Turner's voice was a dry rasp. It was barely audible.

"You bastard. You've got no proof. I don't know what you're talking about."

"You really are the most stubborn man. Allow yourself to tell me the truth. You'll feel much better."

"What truth. Your truth? So you can kill me? You got nothing on me. I wasn't there."

"Ah Mister Turner, I'm afraid you underestimate me. I am somewhat of an expert in finding the truth. You would not be here if I had any doubts. Allow me to show you some of my research."

Koboyashi leant down to retrieve something about the size of a basketball from the floor. Gently he rolled it on to the hotplate. It began to sizzle and crackle. Turner looked at the rotting face that was staring back at him.

"Jesus Christ."

"I can see that I don't need to introduce yourself to your old friend, Mister Turner. Poor Sheriff McLeod. It can be so hard to learn that you weren't above the law after all. We had such a long and interesting conversation about his rather unpleasant urges. Eventually your name came up…"

"He's a filthy liar…"

"Oh, I don't think so. He knew so many details about you that we were able to double-check."

"A man will say anything to save his own skin."

"That is correct, and I was very careful to make it clear that nothing he said would achieve such a result. I work hard to find the truth and nothing as simple as a condemned man's mutterings are ever enough on their own to provide it. Trust me. I know that he was not lying."

Turner grimaced. The pain that he felt was almost unbearable, but he didn't want to give his tormentor the satisfaction of hearing him scream. He bit his lip so hard that it bled.

"Alright. So I was there. I'm a businessman and this sick bastard paid me well. I didn't like the job, but beggars can't be choosers, you know. You happy now? You have your precious truth. Now let me walk."

Koboyashi laughed.

"Ah, this is the teppanyaki of truth, my friend, but it is not the teppanyaki of mercy."

"I can pay you. I can find money."

"Such a shame you spoil your new-found honesty with lies. It doesn't matter though. This is not about money."

"What then? This is about revenge? What the hell has it got to do with you?"

"Now it is my turn to be honest. This is not about money or revenge."

The chef smiled and picked up the serrated knife. He walked around the table and pushed it gently between Turner's two top ribs and started sawing. This time nothing could have stopped Turner from screaming and he did so at the top of his voice. Koboyashi continued talking as if nothing untoward was happening.

"This is my story. Don't worry, it isn't long. When I was a child in Japan there was a huge earthquake. The building that I was in collapsed and trapped my brother and I under a huge pile of rubble."

Having cut through the skin and the muscle binding the bones in Turner's chest, he discarded the knife. The arms of his crisp white shirt were now stained with blood, but he continued calmly.

"I was lucky not to be crushed but Takeshi, my brother, was killed instantly. His body was smashed into pieces. Anyway… there was a great deal of destruction in the city and the rescuers were very busy. After four days we had still not been found."

Turner whimpered.

"It may be hard to believe, looking at me now, but I was a very fat child. I was hungry all the time, and as you can imagine, after four days I was starving. I had no choice but to eat Takeshi."

Koboyashi forced his fingers in between two ribs and pulled them apart. Turner groaned and his remaining eye fluttered wildly. His arms and legs shook against the restraints.

"At first I was disgusted with myself… horrified even. It could not be helped though. I had to eat. After two more days, I realised that the taste was not so bad. In fact, Takeshi was quite delicious."

Koboyashi plunged a hand into Turner's chest.

"It came to pass that, finally, I ate my brother's heart. Never had I experienced anything with a flavour so wonderful."

Black liquid gushed from Turner's mouth as Koboyashi rooted around inside him.

"When I became a cook years later, I tried hearts from many different animals, but I could never reproduce that taste. I was very upset. I was not a bad man, and I didn't want to become one, but I was haunted by the flavour that I was missing. One morning I woke up with the solution to my problem. The world is full of people who deserve to die! Instead of being a monster, I could be a hero!"

With a tug he pulled Turner's still beating heart free and threw it onto the hotplate. It spat and sizzled as it beat for the final time.

"And that, my friend, is the only truth that really matters."

BEFORE THE MEAT TIME

The summer sun is shining down on the garden. The excited sounds made by the other children playing fill the air. I am opening the last of my birthday presents, sitting on the grass, watched by my happy parents. It is my fourth birthday and this is as good as it gets. My new puppy, yet to be named, nuzzles me with its small wet nose and I jump up. Together we run back and forth, lost in the innocence of the moment. I can smell cake and honeysuckle, freshly mowed lawn and… Suddenly I realize that the little dog is no longer running with me. Puzzled, I stop and look around. Where is he? I spot him where the ground curves down to meet the boundary fence, sniffing something that he has found under a bush. With a joyous squeal I run down to meet him.

As soon as I see the rotting cat I start screaming. Its dank matted fur is awash with wriggling maggots. One eye has completely gone and something is moving in the empty socket. I am vaguely aware of my Mother running towards me calling my name. I turn to meet her, arms raised ready to be lifted into her embrace. She bends down towards me but there is something wrong with her face. Her skin is gray green, mottled with streaks of black. One of her eyes is blind, pure white and unblinking. Her mouth hangs open revealing a haphazard row of broken and discolored teeth. Pink drool covers her chin, strands of it swinging thickly below, getting closer and closer. I close my eyes for a moment.

I'm in the now and it is me standing over a little girl. She's practically catatonic with fear, eyelids flickering and lip trembling. As I reach for her I look at my hands. They are covered with dried gore, barely any skin showing. My fingers are twisted into a claw. On one nail I can see the faintest flecks of pink, remnants of the polish I applied in what seems like another life entirely. I only pause for a second before the hunger takes over. The beast inside pushes me aside and without warning…

I'm walking away from the school dining hall. My belly feels swollen and full. My friends, Lucy and Clarissa, are giggling and chatting as we walk down the corridor. The smell of the varnish used to polish the wooden floors is making me nauseous. Their words wash over me as we pass the faded paintings of ex headmasters and glass cabinets full of tarnished sports cups.

"Did you see him watching you? He definitely fancies you."

"Well I don't fancy him. He's a weirdo."

"Says you."

My companions collapsed into laughter, seemingly unaware that I wasn't joining them in their hilarity.

"I think I'm going to be sick," I mumble.

They watch as I accelerate, half running towards the toilets. I push people aside as I go, unbothered by their complaints. Before I reach my destination a large figure steps in front of me and grasps my arm. It is my housemaster, Mr Wells, a rosy-cheeked balding septuagenarian with weight and body odour issues. His voice quivers as he speaks.

"I need to talk to you," he intones.

I struggle in his grip, desperate to get away. I rake his cheek with my fingernails, drawing deep red lines across his wrinkled cheek. He doesn't react.

"Let me go!"

He doesn't. Instead he simply grabs my other arm and holds me there. A faint smell of scotch reaches me with just a touch of stale tobacco.

"I've had a phone call, I'm afraid it's not good news. There has been an accident, a most terrible accident. Your father…"

"No…"

"Yes, I'm afraid your father and mother have been…"

"No. Please…"

"Yes. Your father and mother are both dead."

"That can't be…"

"Your father and mother and your grandparents. Oh, and your brothers too. Also all your cousins and that nice Mrs McCarthy from next door. Now let me think. Everybody that you went to school with…"

I look around. All of the students, who had just a moment before been animated and alive, now lay motionless on the floor. The silence was deafening.

"No!"

Finally I broke free from Mr Wells' grip and ran.

"Everybody is dead. Everybody…"

I slammed open the toilet door just as the contents of my stomach purged themselves. I hung over the basin, gasping and retching until there was nothing more. Breathing heavily, I looked up at the mirror that stretched wall to wall. My hair was tangled and wild and my mascara smudged by my tears. Struggling to focus I blinked.

When I opened my eyes again the mirror was reflecting a monster. My once perfect nose was now little more than a smear of cartilage, hardly visible amidst the other carnage that had been wrought on my face. One side had been torn open, the flap of dry flesh curling back to reveal the inside of my mouth. Around my swollen red eyes a spider's web of cracks and crevasses formed an arid landscape. The disconnect between what I saw in the filthy glass and my own self-image made my knees buckle. I ran my twisted digits over the thick layer of crusted grime that covered my face, feeling a moment of confusion before my consciousness was pushed aside by the beast.

This bathroom was far removed from the refined environs of my former place of learning. Dirt and detritus were everywhere. An inactive neon light stretched across the ceiling, illuminating nothing. A pair of high windows let in a modicum of light but it still remained dim in this stinking toilet. A familiar stench drifted over the stronger smells of industrial cleaning products and effluent, the reek of fear. Clearly I was in this place for a reason and these days there was only one impulse driving my life; hunger.

I shuffled over to the trio of cubicles that lined the back wall. Clumsily I walked into the first, bouncing off the frame. With a low groan I did the same with the second. It swung open and I almost fell into the disgusting morass emerging from the toilet. As I clumsily backed away I could clearly hear whimpering coming from the final stall. Immediately I started battering the locked door with a series of uncoordinated charges. On the fourth or fifth impact the lock gave way and I was face to face with my prey.

Of course it wasn't really 'my' prey. It belonged to the thing that shared my head, the thing that had taken my body for itself. The things that I saw, the terrible things that I did, all seemed to be happening in some kind of everlasting dream. My memories were more real to me than the present. They were visceral and true, as this hunter's existence never could be. Sometimes I would struggle to focus and try to regain control of my actions but my hijacker was stronger and would brook no revolution from me.

"Please, don't… don't kill me. Please…"

It appeared that lunch was a young man, no more than eighteen or nineteen, dressed in jeans and a Coke t-shirt. He glistened with sweat.

"You could let me go. You could…"

He looked around for an escape route but I could see that the fight had already left him. It was one of the peculiarities of killing, that the victim so often ushered in the inevitable before their fate had been written in stone. A well placed shove, a quick burst for freedom… actions that at least gave them some chance to prolong their lives a little, paths not taken. This one was already food walking. I grasped him by the ears and pulled him up to my level.

"No, please…"

I'd like to be able to say that the me, the real me, that resided as prisoner in my own body, would have preferred to look away. Truth be told, it was like watching a train wreck, the horror of the inevitable just couldn't be ignored. I had no choice anyway so I just let the front row view wash over me, partially grateful for the break from my mundane existence.

The first few bites weren't enough to kill him but he slumped in my grip anyway. He twitched and whined as blood poured from the lacerations my teeth had made in his face. Pushing one thumb into an eye socket, to keep him still, I leant into his neck and tore out a chunk of his jugular. Warm salty fluid filled my mouth and that was the end of any restraint that I may have been capable of. I let his corpse slump to the floor and knelt before having my fill of his flesh. Soon my face was covered in a thick layer of viscera, filling my nostrils and sticking my eyelids together. I force them open and shut, my vision flutters.

"So, then the boss said I was one of his best workers and that I could probably make it to manager one day if I kept my head on straight. I was pretty pleased with that. A couple of years with my nose to the grindstone and I could be on 30K. That's pretty decent money…"

The voice droned on and on. We were sitting in a run down Italian restaurant, all red drapes and crimson carpets. A couple of elderly waiters hovered at the edge of the room with disinterest written all over their wrinkled faces. It smelled of stale wine and sweat. I looked closer at my date, because that was clearly what this was, but I didn't recognize him. I'd suffered a lot of pointless dinners like this one, listening, as what had seemed a good idea quickly turned into a bad one. Was this pasty faced individual actually someone I had wasted an evening with? Had I genuinely thought that this was going to be a pleasant romantic experience? It didn't matter really; he fitted a familiar template either way.

"I said, shall we have a drink at the bar before we move on?"

I shrugged and we stood. One of the ancients served us with a couple of bottles of Peroni and we sipped them in silence, watching the other couples as they ate at their tables. There was a commotion as an inebriated group of males burst in, singing some tuneless football anthem. They stormed the bar, demanding refreshment. Immediately I sensed my companion tense up. He looked at the newcomers and scowled, his fingers tightening around his drink.

"Morons," he whispered, not quite as quietly as would have been sensible.

"Sorry mate? Did you say something?"

One of them lumbered over to us. He was a head higher than my date and I couldn't help but notice that he was considerably more handsome. He looked down at us.

"Sorry mate, did you say something?"

The bottle was broken and its jagged end heading for trouble before I could manage a squawk of protest. Its intended victim easily sidestepped it, bringing down a huge fist as he did so. His friends swarmed around us, shouting and waving their arms. The old man behind the bar produced a baseball bat that looked like it had seen better days and started swinging. I was buffeted back and forth before a stray elbow sent me flying back into the nearest table. As I sprawled across an unfortunate couple's dinner, I saw red and snatched up a fork. With an ungraceful wriggle I squirmed back onto my feet and charged. A wall of flesh enveloped me. My weapon was quickly knocked out of my hand and I ricocheted back and forth, unable to see anything but a wall of torsos. A fist hit my temple and I bounced off another body and on to the floor. I pulled myself back up.

We were packed into the narrow corridor, an army of shuffling and groaning creatures joined together by our blood lust. There must have been a dozen of us. It was these moments that I found the oddest, when we became members of the herd. There was certainly no love lost between us. Were there nothing else to eat we would tear each other apart, but the hunt was a different thing. One could sense something primeval in our instinctively consensual mission, something unfettered by societal niceties. We were in this together and it felt right.

As we proceeded, accompanied by our own low growling and the occasional guttural screech, I looked around at my companions. Physically we were a disparate bunch. An extremely overweight teen was to my right, his sweatpants, filthy t-shirt and bare feet suggesting that he had come from his bed. His flabby face had numerous fetid holes in it where others had decided to taste his flesh. In front of me was a much older man, smartly dressed in a dark suit that was now covered in offal. His silver haired head twitched as he walked, and he would turn to look at me, revealing an expression of pure pain. Half of the skin and sinews on his face had been torn away leaving nothing but bone. To his right was a middle-aged woman, resplendent in knitted cardigan emblazoned with a picture of a wolf. One of its, and her, arms had been torn off, leaving a stump of bone emerging from the woolly hole. She was particularly uncoordinated, hitting the wall with one step, and then the old man with another.

I wondered if they were in the same boat as me, still carrying their past consciousness as unwilling passengers on this endless hell ride. There seemed no logical reason that I should be the only one. I looked for some kind of clue in their eyes, a spark of intelligence perhaps. There was none. For the thousandth time I tried to force a meaningful word from my throat but it was beyond me. It bemused and frustrated me, to think that, far from being the end of humanity, we had all just become permanent tourists, cut off from each other as we lurched from one place to another. There were millions, perhaps billions, of us, solitary yet bound together by the same curse.

The corridor widened before leading us into a much bigger space. It seemed to be some kind of warehouse. There were many more of us here, all held in thrall by the smell of life. I heard the dull thud of gunshots but it was a full minute before my head happened to turn towards the shooters. There were half a dozen of the living, perched on top of a shipping crate, four adults and two kids. The kids looked terrified and… delicious? I ran that thought over in my head again. It seemed wrong but I couldn't separate the two ideas. I joined the baying crowd in orbiting the elevated food. We hissed and growled at each other but our dead hearts weren't in it. We only wanted to eat.

In front of me, someone's head exploded. The corpse took a couple of steps before collapsing onto the ground. The boom of the shotgun was as dull as the pain that I suddenly felt tear across my arm. I staggered but didn't fall. A second shot tore into my knee and this time I went over, hitting the ground hard. Others tripped over me as I tried unsuccessfully to get up on a leg that would no longer support my weight. Another shot hit one of my fellow undead causing him or her, I couldn't see which, to fall across my chest and I was trapped.

I lay there staring up at the swirling crowd. The dim overhead lights seemed to flash on and off as my view became blocked and then clear again. Something had caught fire and a pirouetting flume of smoke drifted across my vision. My senses started to blur together.

It was the disco. The stench of sweat and poppers conspiring with the thumping beats to make my head throb. Black-eyed partygoers lurched from place to place, their limbs vibrating to the music. It was oppressive and I could take no more of it. My friends, more like acquaintances to be honest, were nowhere to be seen. Grabbing my coat from the cloakroom I climbed the steep steps that led out to the cold clear night.

Gulping the fresh air I headed up the small side street hoping to flag down a passing taxi. As I reached the main road someone ran past. Surprised, I stopped. Then two more rushed by. As I puzzled this a group of six or seven more rushed by me. One was screaming. Tentatively I walked up to the junction and looked out. Before I knew it they were on me. The first pinned me to the ground, snarling at the others as he staked his claim.

"Get the hell off me," I shouted, more outraged than frightened, pummeling his arms with my fists.

As the stench washed over me and I took a proper look at the wounds on the side of his head, I started to realize that this was more than just a drunken student going too far. This was something other, something that shouldn't be happening outside of a nightmare. It was then that I screamed. He sank his teeth into my neck. I writhed underneath him for a moment but as his cold saliva mixed with my warm blood I felt a new calm come over me. I could feel the life leaving me but with it went the panic, the worries, all of the human frailties that usually accompanied me from minute to minute. As my skin tightened and dried all over my body, I was reborn.

I remember the days before the meat time.

There was once a world where people didn't think of each other as food. A world where there was more to existence than tearing the flesh from each other's bones. Unbelievable as it now sounds, there was respect, kindness and even love. Of course humanity requires, well, humans… and there are few of those left now. We are the darkness and we are all that remains.

HOPE
ETERNAL

It wasn't that he considered the other residents of the hostel to be evil. He didn't think that they intended him harm, or even that they harbored wicked intentions toward him. It was more that they carried an air of decay, the ghosts of their loss almost tangible in this dimly lit chamber. Their pale faces and sunken cheeks, their fading eyes, all sent a shiver of discomfort down his aching spine. His own grief haunted him enough. To accommodate or in any way absorb the sadness of strangers would soon have broken him.

This greasy table at which he sat was a centerpiece to a room devoid of colour. The grey walls were decorated only by dirt and dust, topped off here and there by a tattered notice, which added nothing to the general ambience. On the floor was the memory of a carpet. The ancient floor covering was so threadbare and full of holes that it had almost merged with the stone on which it rested.

The resident stench was genuinely repulsive. Ancient black mould and persistent damp gave the air a sharp tang which you could taste, while the omnipresent and odorous unwashed added their own resolute stink. His nose twitched constantly in protest. Chambers sighed and pushed his plate of half eaten 'stew' away from him. More depressing than every other aspect of this dismal place was that he belonged here as much as any man.

"Are you going to eat that?"

A spindly figure installed himself into the chair opposite. Even if Chambers hadn't been familiar with the man's phlegmatic voice, the request could not have come from anyone else. Sullivan was a master scrounger. No crumb was wasted when he was present, which he always seemed to be. Despite this he was skeletal, host to some creeping pestilence that Chambers had little desire to know about.

"No. Help yourself."

"Thanks," muttered Sullivan, his first spoon of the brown mush already nearly in his mouth. "Are you going out tonight?"

Chambers grunted and got to his feet. He had no time for small talk these days. He simply couldn't find any enthusiasm for it. After retrieving his coat from the back of his chair, he left the man to his scraps.

A small crowd loitered around the hostel entrance, smoking and bantering as idle men do. The back and forth was merely meant to raise their spirits but their false optimism only worsened Chamber's dull sense of despair. Taking a deep breath he stepped out into the cold dusk, pulling on his coat and hat as he did so. There was a sudden lull in conversation as the men turned their attention to him.

"Alright Chambers? Fancy spending an evening underground with us for a change?"

"Chambers is indestructible. He don't need to hide."

"Leave 'im alone, he's got his reasons."

Chambers gave them a slow nod and walked off into the gloom. The streets were busy with people heading for shelter, eager to survive for another night. He pulled his hat down further and threaded himself through the crowd, avoiding eye contact as he went against the flow.

His wound throbbed as he walked but he didn't allow himself to wince. He was lucky to still have two legs, as his surgeon had made sure to tell him on several occasions. Indeed, he was lucky to be alive at all when so many others weren't. Of course luck was relative, and in the scheme of things he didn't feel fortunate, but he did consider it unconscionable to complain about his lot, even if it was only to himself.

They had survived a solid week of fighting in and around a devastated French town. It had been bloody and intense but without the disorienting openness of the field. Plunged back into 'la campagne' he had felt weightless, unable to acclimatize away from the familiarity of bricks and mortar.

On their second day in nature a mine had liquefied two men, not ten feet in front of them. It had torn their bodies into nothingness, leaving only a stain as proof that they had ever even existed. As well as coating him in the viscera of his friends it had sent a shard of shrapnel into his right leg. In a sense, such as could only be so in a world gone mad, this had been a godsend; a blessing. The damage was great enough to grant him escape from the bloody killing fields. He could see the hint of jealousy in the expressions of those that had lifted him up and stretchered him away. Had he not been screaming in pain, he might even have apologized for being the recipient of such fortuity.

Of course neither he nor they could have known that his hopes were being raised falsely, that this glimmer of light would soon be extinguished. He supposed that they had broken the news as gently as they could, but in reality there was no good way to tell someone such a thing. Besides, he was just one of a multitude awash in this sea of suffering drowning humanity the world over.

"Private Chambers? My name is Father Calum. I'm afraid I have some extremely unfortunate news. We have received notice that your wife was killed in an air raid. Her body was identified yesterday."

He had stared at the chaplain in disbelief, a white noise rapidly filling his head. Her first visit since he had returned from Europe had been scheduled for that very afternoon.

"Are you sure?" His voice was wet gravel. "Could it be some kind of mistake?"

"I'm sorry. They rarely make mistakes in cases like this. They like to be sure before sending out any kind of notification. Most probably she was carrying her papers or a neighbor identified the… the body."

"What about my daughter? I need to know about my daughter."

He grasped the chaplain's wrist tightly as he spoke.

"Daughter? I'm sorry but there's no mention of her in the paperwork. I'll make enquiries for you. Could she have been elsewhere? With grandparents perhaps?"

Chambers had released the priest and slumped back onto his bed. His father died in the fight for the Somme; his mother had never recovered from the loss and spent the next two decades fading away gradually. She had been little more than a shadow by the time that she died. His wife's mother had died in childbirth and her father had died from cirrhosis of the liver as the war broke.

"No. No, there's nobody else."

"I'm sorry to hear that. Still, I'll pass on the word. Don't lose hope."

Of course no news had been forthcoming. Nobody had seen nor heard from little Rose; as far as anyone could tell she had simply vanished. As soon as he had been able to walk he had made his escape and headed for London; he would conduct his own search. He spent a full week picking through the rubble of their flattened terrace home but had found nothing except for the detritus of their former lives. Finally satisfied that he had exhausted that possibility he turned to the hospitals and morgues.

They were a litany of the dead and dying. It crushed his soul to see how much his city, his people, had suffered. Day after day he had been awash in the miasma of death; day after day he forced one foot in front of another as he toured past an endless parade of shell-shocked faces. His daughter was nowhere to be found but still he couldn't bring himself to give up on her. London was his home and, despite his physical and mental exhaustion, he belonged here; his search had to continue.

As darkness fell he limped on through the increasingly empty streets. All around him was desolation; buildings either reduced to rubble or bearing open wounds that left their interiors exposed to the elements. Yet there was still strength left in the city. She was reeling from the blows that she had suffered but she was not out for the count just yet. Across the ragged vista he could see St Paul's, untouched and proud. The Tower and countless other stone witnesses to history continued to watch grimly while the war rolled on.

To be a Londoner, mere flesh and bone, was to be a part of this place. He felt it deep down, a belonging that engendered fury when he looked out at the damage inflicted by the German warplanes. When he thought about the pilots flying from their homes to attack his, he didn't consider them to be sent by man. Like him they fought for their cities, the ancients grown to vastness from humble beginnings. What had once been a smattering of rough dwellings, created by humans, had grown to a point where destiny could not be dictated by one as small as him, where their survival was more important in the long run. Mankind had become willing servants, eager to escape nature's barbaric reign and strive for 'civilisation'. The cities rewarded them as they saw fit.

"Hey you! What do you think you're doing? Get off the streets."

The air warden in his white helmet ran over from the other side of the road.

"Bloody hell, not you again. I should have known. You know the drill, get to a shelter."

Chambers looked at him and nodded, unwilling to repeat the fruitless arguments that he had tried on their previous encounters. He turned and ambled back in the direction from which he had come, and, once out of sight, turned a side street and doubled back.

Only moments later the dolorous wail of sirens broke

the night's silence. Spotlights shot beams of intense light up into the cloudy skies, sweeping across each other in their search for the invaders. Derek Chambers stood and watched, straining to see if it was a false alarm. It made little difference to him either way; he was a man on a mission, however hopeless that may be. In that respect he had tunnel vision and could not be deterred.

He had asked himself if he feared dying and found that he did not. Whether it was having survived his own brush with death, or his wife's terminal appointment with it, he did not know. It wasn't that he no longer knew fear, it was that it had become a stationary thing, resident yet unmoving. There just came a point where it served no purpose and, as long as you managed to avoid catching its gaze, it could be largely ignored.

The open fields of France had terrified him during every waking moment. He had felt exposed and displaced, sure that a bullet would plunge him into eternal darkness at any moment. Oddly, bullets aside, it had reminded him of childhood visits to the countryside with his frail Mother. He had hated it and only relaxed once he was back home in amidst the familiar sights and sounds of London. Knowing that there were strangers looking to kill him had shredded his nerves, but little more than the open skies and ever-stretching horizon. Now though, at this moment, where mortality was concerned, he was entirely relaxed.

He sensed something moving on the bombsite behind him and span around. He peered into the shadows, unwilling to use his torch. He didn't want to get himself arrested. A darker shadow seemed to dart across the remains of the house's back wall.

"Rose?" he called in a shouted whisper.

Nothing.

He clambered over piles of brick and splintered wood towards the source of his curiosity. His leg protested vigorously at his exertions but he ignored it.

"Rose?"

He stopped to listen. The steady drone of incoming bombers could be heard clearly now. They were soon joined by the rattle of anti-aircraft guns sending glowing pulses of flak up into the clouds. He shuddered, more from the cold than anything else, and looked back to where he thought he had seen something. There was nothing there.

"Hell."

The horizon lit up with explosions as the first bombs began to hit. A few fell closer and then they were everywhere, birthing towers of fire across the city. He could hear them whistling and screeching as they fell, plummeting down with no discernable pattern. The air was thick with dust and smoke, and the smell of burning timber and cordite. He couldn't see more than a foot in front of him, such was the swirling chaos in which he stood.

He was nearing the end of his second month under the Blitz. They came every night without fail, those murderers in their flying machines, and every night they tried to kill him. He had stood in the face of their devastation and waited for them to do their worst; again and again they had failed. Once they were gone he would wake from an almost meditative state and march on across the broken glass and hot ground in search of his lost child.

Tonight began no differently to any other. As the sounds and smells of this earthly hell cocooned him, blocking any kind of normal sensory input, he had drifted off to that inner place where the ghosts of his recent past spoke to him. The experience reminded him of watching newsreels, except in this case they were personal to him and somewhat fleeting. The memories were bitter sweet; John and Frank the night before they had died in that bloody field, his poor emaciated mother and her sad smile.

"Watch out Derek. Here it comes." It was his wife's voice, calm and reassuring.

A wave of heat rolled over him followed, by a force that blew him head over heels. He was thrown across the rubble and into a deep black void. When he woke it was still night but the raid was over. His head buzzing, he picked himself up gingerly from the floor. His face felt wet and when he touched it, his fingers came away covered with a slick of blood. He wiped his eyes with the back of his sleeve and blinked, his eyelids sticky and his sight blurred.

Something moved in his peripheral vision and he turned to try and focus on it. He squinted into the shadows.

"Daddy."

Had he actually heard the voice or was it just the wind? The night was full of distant sounds following the raid. He couldn't be sure. His head throbbed as he took a few stumbling steps towards where he thought he had seen something. He stood gazing into the black for several long minutes but there really was nothing there anymore, if there ever had been. Eventually a hand on his shoulder brought him back to his surroundings.

"That's a nasty cut you got there. Looks like a bleeder. I'm not saying it isn't bad but that kind of head wound always look worse than it is."

The speaker was an extremely old man. He wore a flat cap and a spotless tweed suit, oddly pristine considering the circumstances. Although his face was a morass of wrinkles and worn skin, his eyes sparkled in the darkness. He rubbed his hands together before shoving them into his pockets.

"I… I think I'm alright. Did you see a little girl?"

"I beg your pardon?"

"Did you see a little girl just over there?"

"No, I…"

"Sorry. I was looking for my daughter. I thought I saw something but I must have imagined it."

"Your daughter? Was she with you?"

"No. No… I lost her, or at least she disappeared. I thought that perhaps… well… it doesn't matter. Please… I'd better be going."

The old man tipped his cap.

"Are you sure you can manage? Your head…"

"Thank you. I'm fine. I'll get some rest. Thank you. Good night."

A thorough cleaning of the wound revealed it to be nothing more than a deep gouge, and unlikely to be life threatening. It might have benefited from stitches but he settled for a whisky and some rest. He was woken hours later by someone shaking his shoulders. It was Sullivan.

"Wake up, there's another raid. I don't know how you can sleep through those sirens."

Swiftly he pulled his boots on and walked out through the empty hostel into the street. Thankfully Sullivan had already scurried away, so he was free to head in the opposite direction. After a near miss with his nemesis, the air warden, he strode on across the rubble with no clear destination in mind. Although his head gave him little trouble, he was aware of how tired he had become, both mentally and physically. He felt constantly one step removed from the world, as if his senses had become worn at the edges.

Hearing the drone of the incoming bombers he looked up and found that he was next to the ruins of a church. The nave had collapsed in on itself, leaving only the tower looming over a cross of bricks and glass. Gravestones had been knocked asunder by the blast and he stopped to read them, although at first the names written on them hardly registered. It was only when he reached the marker for a small child, similar in age to his own, that he allowed the information to sink in. This bloody war, he thought, this bloody war.

Although not much of a one for proverbs, even though his mother had lived by them, lightning never striking the same place twice had always resonated with him. Had he noticed the unexploded bomb, or been conscious long enough to note the detonation, he might have allowed himself a certain measure of satisfaction. As it was, the explosion threw him across the rubble like a rag doll.

"Open your eyes, daddy."

"Rose? Is that you?"

She stood over him, offering her hand. He took it and pulled himself to his feet.

"Of course it's me, silly. Who else would it be?"

"I… but where have you been? I've missed you. I've been looking for you, you know."

"We've missed you too."

"We?"

"Mummy and me. We've been waiting for you."

"But Mummy…"

Rose let go of his hand and skipped away from him. He realized now that she was not entirely opaque. As she turned he caught glimpses of moonlight passing through her.

"Are you…"

He felt a sudden intense pain in his chest and for a split second his daughter disappeared.

"Daddy?"

"Rose…"

The pain came again and he gasped for breath, newly aware that his lungs were empty. Once more Rose vanished and then reappeared. She was fully transparent now and he could see the churchyard behind her.

"Daddy, don't go…"

He was overcome by a pain that seemed to encompass his whole body. Sparkling lights filled his vision and when they eventually cleared, he found that he was lying on the floor. The Air Warden was kneeling next to him, pushing down on his chest. A Priest stood nearby with an anxious expression.

"He's back."

"You bloody fool. You're lucky to be alive."

Chambers sat upright.

"Rose."

"Who?"

"My daughter. She was here a moment ago."

"We haven't seen anyone else."

"Help me up."

"You should stay still. You're hurt. You were a dead man."

Chambers scrabbled to his feet. He ached all over but couldn't find any specific injury. The Warden grabbed his arm.

"You need to rest."

He shook him off.

"I need to go."

He lurched away, leaving his bemused rescuers behind. His journey back to the hostel was a blur, his focus only returning as he pushed back the crowd of smokers taking in the evening air.

"Back from your constitutional, Chambers?"

"Are you alright Chambers? You're a mess."

Inside it was quiet and nobody disturbed him as he headed out to the back, where the lockers were. With shaking hands he opened his and took out a small bundle. It struck him that, for the first time in what felt like an eternity, he felt at peace. After so long it was an odd sensation. Smiling to himself he went into the toilets and locked himself into a cubicle. He sat down and carefully unwrapped his prize.

The gun seemed to gleam as he unwrapped it. It had saved his life on various occasions and he considered it to be an old friend. He exhaled.

"Here I come my darlings, here I come."

He put the barrel into his mouth and pulled the trigger.

THE LAST PATROL

The fat man leant back and drained the whiskey bottle dry. With a groan of satisfaction he licked his lips before pulling himself up and onto his feet.

"Goddamn," he muttered, slamming the empty vessel down onto a pile of boxes masquerading as a makeup table. "You know," he slurred in a deep voice still redolent of good breeding and an expensive education, "I saw him without the paint once."

The boy eyed him warily. "No, you never did."

He had lost count of how many times he'd heard this lie.

They looked at each other dolefully. Outside the wind and rain continued to thrash the small tent without mercy. Puddles of water were gathering around the edges of the canvas walls and the air was damp and cold. Somewhere in the distance an angry lion roared.

Without warning the entrance flap was flung aside. The newcomer was just over six feet tall and of solid build. A razor sharp crew cut sat atop a chiseled face painted with green and orange stripes. His skin glistened with moisture from the downpour. He glanced around the tent with black eyes more akin to those of an animal than a man, saw no strangers, and then visibly relaxed.

"Boy. Doc."

The older man nodded in greeting, one corner of his orange lips turning up slightly.

"Good to see you Sarge."

The youth nodded and shuffled his feet silently.

"It's looking ugly out there."

Sarge wandered over to the makeshift clothes rail that they had constructed from a couple of pitchforks and a length of rope. He peeled off his khaki t-shirt, revealing a muscled torso patterned with burn scars and a livid pink line stretching from neck to navel. The butt of a Colt Commander protruded from the waistband of his combat trousers. The others watched as he pulled it out and dropped it onto the floor before selecting a bright green satin jumpsuit with fluffy white buttons and cuffs. Outside there was a crash of thunder and the storm stepped up a notch.

The boy cleared his throat.

"I was thinking about the routine..."

Sarge cut him short, his expression grim.

"We don't change the plan. It's worked so far and that's good enough for me."

He kicked off his mud splattered combat boots and stepped into the suit before shrugging it over his arms.

"Now zip me up."

Doc watched them for a moment, lost in thought. He turned away and stared into the cracked mirror nestled amongst the discarded tubs of powder and paint. Red eyes and a bloated white face stared back at him. The years hadn't been kind and his reflection disgusted him. With a sigh he turned his attention to straightening his enormous yellow Afro wig.

"Got any of your specials, Doc? I need something to pick me up."

"Here's your case."

The boy ran over to scoop it up from a brown pool of muddy water.

Doc settled the battered black bag on his knee and undid the bronze clasp. He peered inside. Where once there would have been order there was now chaos. Brown pill bottles lay strewn amongst surgical instruments that had seen better days. He selected one marked 'Dexamphetamine' that nestled in the grasp of a pair of plasma flecked obstetrical forceps. Sarge took it and popped the lid before upending it into his mouth.

"Has anyone checked the Jeep? I don't want a repeat of last time."

Sarge shuddered, leaning down to retrieve his boots and pistol.

"I think Jones checked it out," Doc offered.

"I hope so. We'll use the same formation as we always do. Boy driving and you on spotlight, Doc. I'll take the main gun."

Doc looked down at his swollen hands, hands that had decided the fate of countless innocents in his previous life. They were trembling.

"Fine. Whatever you say."

The boy nodded agreement. "Sure."

"Good. Now, where the hell is my nose?"

The Jeep had seen better days but Jones, the Circus handyman, did the best that he could with it. A coating of white paint and purple polka dots concealed filled bullet holes surprisingly well. Fur seat covers did an admirable job of keeping the ingrained bloodstains out of sight. A spotlight had been welded on to the machine-gun mounting and a compressed air powered cannon shot confetti from the rear.

The trio ducked into the backstage area, shaking off the rain as they entered. Sarge looked at the jeep, cast in shadow, and sighed. He could still see the cracked paint and torn seats. He could still see the ghosts, still hear their screams and smell their burning flesh.

"OK men, buckle up. It's show time."

They took their places silently and sat listening as the muffled sounds of the arena washed over them. The boy wiped his hands on his tartan trousers nervously. His teeth chattered in the cold. He hated waiting. He'd spent too many years waiting in vain for someone to rescue him from the clutches of those wretched nuns.

"Start her up..."

In the main arena the music built to a crescendo and came to an end. The crowd roared and out marched half a dozen sweat soaked Chinese knife throwers. Automatically Sarge covered their movements with the cannon. All except one ignored him but their leader stopped for a moment and met his gaze. He was an intimidating individual with a furious stare and tattoos of snarling Dragons that covered both arms. Time flickered for a moment as the two men in silk weighed each other up in the semi-darkness, eyes blazing and lips curled.

"We are go!" screeched the boy, as two emaciated girls in sparkling leotards pulled back the sheets covering the entrance. Sarge drew his finger across his throat before turning away as the engine roared into action.

"Entrance of the Gladiators" blasted out of the PA and the lights dimmed as the boy swung them into an orbit along the arena's periphery. Doc bit his lip and sent the spotlight arcing across the crowd. Fragments of faces and body parts were illuminated momentarily by its glare. His grip tightened around the rubberised handles as he looked out at the multitude, inspecting them for imperfections, evaluating their suitability for surgery. They stared back, unaware of the mental dissection that they were undergoing.

He wondered if they were in Massachusetts; or even worse perhaps they were actually in Boston. He had found that it helped his nerves to be unaware of where the circus was playing. Of course it wasn't always possible to avoid finding out but alcohol and tranquilisers helped him remain unconscious and oblivious much of the time.

Boston. There were a lot of people in that city who would love to get their hands on him. Sometimes he would dream that they had finally caught up with him and that the roles had become reversed. He would see himself strapped to the operating table while they crowded around him, their faces hidden by surgical masks. As they leant down over him with their scalpels at the ready he would try to scream, but the anesthetic wouldn't let him.

It had seemed unfair that he had received so many death threats during the court case. After all, the jury had come to the conclusion that he wasn't responsible for his actions.

Nobody actually knew whom he had deliberately helped to die. It was between him and the Creator and not the domain of lesser mortals. The voices had assured him that he was on the side of good, saving the chosen from future wretchedness and suffering. He'd had the sense not to share that information with anybody, especially not that erroneously self-righteous Judge, and silence had earned him a relatively fortunate verdict.

After serving his spell in the sanatorium he had not gone back. His time spent with the criminally insane could not be described as pleasant but it had been informative. He had learnt that he didn't belong amongst the complacent and comfortable. He told himself that no one knew who he had been, that nobody could possibly recognise him dressed as he was. Still, his mouth was dry as he stared out at the crowd.

Overhead, the lighting operator switched everything to green, just as two enormous mortars fired shredded silver paper in a plume over the crowd. Sarge blinked, attempting to clear the salt lacing his eyes. For a moment he thought he saw paratroopers descending from above but shook off the hallucination and turned his attention to the stalls. A group of youngsters were caught by Doc's spotlight for a split second, their eyes wide with wonderment and a touch of fear.

It was enough to send Sarge back to the jungle, back to the children in the village. Their eyes had been the same, gazing up at him intently, even after he had slaughtered them with his bayonet and laid them all out in a row. At the time it had seemed the kind thing to do, a mercy killing of sorts. After all they had executed everyone else, so who would have looked after them? There was something complete about leaving them lying peacefully amongst the burning buildings. It had been a

Zen moment.

The jungle was a rebirth for him. He had been an overgrown boy of twenty-one when the call came. His ambition had been to be a comic actor of all things, something that seemed impossible to imagine now. A seemingly endless stream of auditions had led to nothing and then Uncle Sam had written demanding his help. For a split second he had wondered about hiding in Canada. The notion was probably just a reflection of the liberal attitudes of those around him but he had thought better of it anyway. He kissed his wife goodbye and took the Greyhound across country, as ordered, to Fort Polk. His heart had swelled with pride when they gave him his uniform, and when he was handed his M16 he had almost fainted with joy.

After basic training he had shipped out and arrived just as the Tet Offensive was at its peak. When they camouflaged his face at Khe Sanh he knew that this was his destiny. This was the only role that he had been born to play. As they crept through the undergrowth, struggling to breathe in the humidity, he was possessed by the muse. Tearing into those villages, deafened by the clatter of their own guns and the screams of their enemies, he had given the performance of his life.

Up front the boy had flicked a switch, sending a thick cloud of red smoke trailing out behind them. Sarge looked at it grimly before priming the release mechanism on the steel canister down by his feet. The jeep completed its first lap and Sarge opened fire. His eyes narrowed as the rainbow projectiles arced out over the crowd.

Doc was hauling himself up onto his seat, using the

spotlight as a lever. Forcing a smile onto his face he let go with one hand and waved at the crowd. The Jeep swerved slightly as they took the corner and he fell onto one knee, hitting his nose on cold steel as he went. Automatically he put his hand to his face and it came away bloody.

"Jesus Christ boy, you'll pay for that."

In the front seat the boy heard nothing. As always his thoughts were elsewhere, fragile images from his past flashing through his mind. His traitorous mother's face blaming him for his father's death; raised fists raining down on him endlessly throughout his time at the orphanage. He blinked as the slideshow continued. Father O'Brian's oily smile as he towered over him; the filthy hobos who offered him shelter and then used him as a diversion from their own empty existences. In his mind's eye he could still see the razor flashing as it unmanned the Godless Priest and eviscerated those faithless drifters. The tiny blade had been his only friend, the only one who ever stood up for him. He still carried it at all times just in case he needed someone to stand up for him again. His knuckles whitened as he gripped the wheel tighter. His foot pushed a little harder on the accelerator.

Sarge had run out of ammunition. The gun in his boot scratched at his ankle, reminding him that it was there. He ignored it and climbed over into the back seat. Doc grinned at him with crimson stained teeth. He shook his head. Sarge stared at him for a moment before turning away and tapping the boy's shoulder. The two men held on as the Jeep decelerated rapidly before coming to a skidding halt in the sawdust. The lights dimmed and a strobe light started up, slicing their movements into stuttering monochrome.

"Out!"

Sarge hit the ground and rolled into a somersault. Doc stood and managed to trip over the edge of the Jeep, landing heavily on his hands. The crowd roared its approval, taking it to be a part of the act. Sarge ran to him and hauled him upright. For a second they stood there looking out at the crowd before jogging in opposite directions around the vehicle. Doc wheezed and spat the occasional gobbet of blood while Sarge ran slowly and steadily, a thousand yard stare on his face.

The boy leant over and retrieved an old-fashioned bulb horn from the passenger foot well. He then extricated himself from behind the wheel and marched over to the audience barrier, swinging his arms as he went. Even though he measured in at over six feet, his head barely reached over the top of the solid wooden wall. So it was that he came face to face with a little girl with blond locks and a dress that should never been seen outside of fairy tales. She stared into his cold blue eyes and found nothing to like. Her bottom lip began to tremble. Adjusting her focus she took in the streaked white face paint and cracked red nose. The tremors spread. For want of anything else to do, the boy unleashed a smile. The sight of his blackened and broken teeth triggered a veritable facial earthquake as she opened her mouth in order to inhale enough oxygen for an ear splitting wail. Before she could start he whipped the horn over the barrier and into her face, unleashing an enormous volley of honking sounds as he did so. He was on his way back to the Jeep before she had even filled her lungs.

Sarge and Doc were still running round in circles but when they saw his approach they stopped and grabbed their ankles. Boy performed a leapfrog maneuver over each of them, squeezing the horn victoriously at the apex of each jump. When he had finished, the trio clambered back into the car.

With Boy putting the pedal to the metal they performed another circuit at breakneck speed. A morose silence hung over them as the music faded before segueing into a drum roll. Having completed their final tour they slowed to a halt once more. Sarge turned to face inwards towards the centre of the arena. He raised his hand in a fist and almost magically a circle of flame appeared in the darkness. Next to it a ramp revealed itself in the firelight.

When he'd returned from in country and discovered that his wife had run off with one of the local cops, Sarge had lost himself in the bottle for a week. Then he picked himself up and made it his business to beat the usurper to a bloody lifeless pulp. It had made perfect sense. If he had learned one thing from the Marine Corp it was how justice worked and right was on his side. Of course he couldn't expect civilians to understand. They were sheep and he was the shepherd. They didn't have to make things right in the world; that was his job. He told his shattered wife that he loved her and then ran. As he ran he saw that the sheep didn't appreciate the hell that he had lived through in order to make their lives possible. In fact they positively denounced it. The enemy had won. They had become us and there was no good left in the world anymore.

Sarge leant over and whispered into the boy's ear. "Do it."

The engine roared as the boy slammed it down a gear and jammed the wheel round anti-clockwise as far as it would go. The music stopped and the crowd fell silent as they hurtled towards the ramp, isolated in the vehicle from the rest of the world. Sarge's fingers twitched, muscle memory recalling the sweet release of a trigger squeeze. Doc locked his hands together as he remembered what it had been like when he had the power of life and death over others. The boy simply screamed as he pushed pedal to metal.

They hit the ramp too fast and too wide and instantly they knew it was all wrong. The vehicle tilted down to one side as they hit the flaming hoop and by the time it hit the floor they were upside down. The boy was thrown clear and landed in a heap to one side.

The first to emerge from the inverted Jeep was Doc. His wig was gone and he was cradling his right arm with the left. His face was a mask of blood, both from his nose and a fresh gash across his forehead. He looked about, seemingly unsure where he actually was, and stumbled forwards a few feet before stopping. He looked back at the four wheels spinning in the air just as a solitary flame licked out across the exposed underside. Startled he stepped back and immediately fell over the boy and landed on his back. His arms and legs waggled in the air for a few seconds before he managed to roll over onto his hands and knees. He looked at the ragged pile in front of him.

"Boy?" Cautiously he turned the body over. It was immediately obvious from the angle of the head that the boy's neck had been broken. A tear rolled down Doc's face paint. "Boy?"

The fire had enveloped the Jeep more thoroughly now but miraculously Sarge emerged from the wreckage in a crawl. The front of his jumpsuit had been torn away and his face was covered in cuts. His conical hat had lost the pom pom from the top, but was managing to cling on to his head despite its battered state. In a crouch he jogged over to Doc and Boy.

Doc looked up at him. "I haven't got my bag, Sarge. Have you seen my bag?"

"It's alright, Doc. It's alright."

From the blackness a group of figures started to emerge. Sarge pulled the Colt from his boot and waved it at them.

"Get the hell back."

Somewhere up near ringside a woman started crying.

A lone figure stepped forwards from the other would be rescuers. It was the leader of the knife-throwing group, his knives now safely tucked into his waistband. He raised his hands over his head.

"We just want to help."

"I said keep the hell back."

"We need to put the fire out, Sarge. If you..."

"Next one is in your head, now stay back."

The shot sent the others scurrying back into the shadows but the knife thrower remained. He stood and watched them, his head bowed slightly.

Doc looked up at Sarge. "Is this the end?"

"We're surrounded. I can't see a way out."

Doc stared at the boy's lifeless face.

"I don't think I can carry on Sarge. I'm done. I hate

to ask you but do you think..."

"Of course."

The bullet did its job instantly and Doc's life left him. He slumped down onto the boy's chest. Sarge took aim at his would be rescuer.

"This has been a long time coming..."

The fuel tank exploded, swiftly followed by the compressed air canister. With a deafening boom a ball of flame expanded outwards and upwards, engulfing and evaporating the trio instantly. When the inferno finally subsided all that remained were unclaimed memories and the sound of one man clapping.

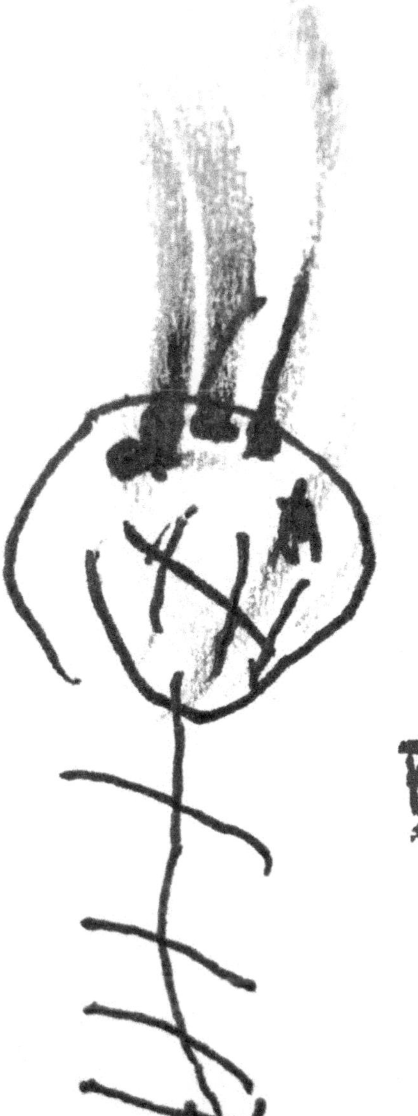

BEYOND THE BOOK

Konrad Bader made slow progress crossing the dim room. At 92 he had lost interest in hurrying. Nothing was that pressing any more. Of course, even if he had wanted to rush then his body wouldn't have co-operated. Surviving for as long as he had came with a price. His ailments were too long to list. If anyone ever asked after his health his curt response was always the same.

"Just a touch of heart failure. Nothing to worry about."

An ancient cat mewed unenthusiastically from atop a teetering stack of old newspapers. Konrad nodded and waved a liver spotted hand in the feline's general direction.

"Not now Arthur, not now."

Finally he reached his writing desk and, with a groan, lowered his aching body onto the attendant chair.

"Computer on."

The display came to life immediately, the familiar glow of Facebook casting a blue light onto his wizened visage.

"Show friends online."

"Zero friends online," replied the machine.

Konrad cursed. Where the hell was Bob? Sleeping probably. Bob was only a few years younger than him and also spent a large part of his day unconscious. Konrad sighed, feeling the spike of anger quickly subside. Bob was the only one of his friends left. They had never actually met but they had known each other through Facebook for the best part of 40 years.

It puzzled him how he, a retired school teacher from Vienna, and Bob, a portly right wing ex truck driver, ever found anything to talk about. But talk they did. Endlessly and on any subject that flitted across their minds.

"Ah well."

Now he was there he might as well have a little browse. He was feeling nostalgic so chose to scroll back through his own personal history. It was an activity that left him morose and regretful, but that he could never resist.

There was the digital memorial to Else, ten years in her grave now. The death of their only son Tom had finished her off; outliving your offspring was another cost of living beyond your allocated innings. There was the anniversary notification marking half a century using this damn site. That had given him pause for thought, for sure. The boy's picture filled the screen, a scrawny teen rather than the pensioner he'd been when he passed, but Konrad kept on scrolling. Old houses, jobs, friends and holidays blurred by as he journeyed back to another time. He watched Tom getting younger and younger until he was only a newborn, pink and tiny in his wife's arms. A picture of him and Else at a rock festival caught his eye.

"Those were the days."

"Incoming video caller. Unknown user."

Konrad paused and then threw caution to the wind.

"Ah, go ahead and accept it."

A balding middle-aged man with a badly trimmed goatee filled the screen. His face was blotchy and his eyes red rimmed. His accent was thick, a classic product of the Southern US.

"Hello? Is that Konrad Bader?"

"Yes. Naturally. How can I help you?"

"Oh. Sorry. You don't know me. My name is Mike; I'm Bob's son. I hate to be the bearer of bad news but I'm afraid my Dad passed away yesterday. He went in his sleep so at least it was quick. Anyway, I know you two used to talk a lot so I thought I'd better let you know. So… there it is. Sorry. Take care now."

Mike ended the call.

A great sorrow came over Konrad. He was now truly alone. Grief stole the very breath from him, a tangible weight on his soul that crushed his heart into eternal stillness. His eyes rolled up in his head, he took his last breath and, with a thump, his head hit the desk. Arthur leapt off his perch and padded over. He rubbed himself against the dead man's ankles, purring gently.

On the screen something strange was happening.

"Ten friends online."

"Fifty friends online."

"Five hundred friends online."

From Konrad's motionless corpse a spectral shadow sat up in the chair and a transparent hand reached out for the mouse. With a ghostly smile he began to click…

ABOUT THE AUTHOR

Andrew Freudenberg is an English author with a German name. He was born in France.

Despite always having a strong love for the written word, he spent a large part of his 20's dabbling in the global techno scene. He loves heavy metal.

A number of his stories have appeared in anthologies, but this is his first solo collection.

He currently lives in the South West of England, with his Ninja wife and three sons.

Previous Publishing History

Something Akin to Despair
Previously Unpublished

A Bitter Parliament
Originally published in 'M v F: Death Personified' – JEA Press 2016

Charlie's Turn
Previously Unpublished

Pater in Tenebris
Originally Published in 'The Black Room Manuscripts Volume Three' – Sinister Horror Company 2018

Milkshake
Originally published in 'Barnyard Horror' – JWK Publishing 2013

Nose to the Window
Previously Unpublished

The Cardiac Ordeal
Originally published in 'Great British Horror 2: Dark Satanic Mills' – Black Shuck Books 2017

Meat Sweets

Originally Published in 'Ugly Babies' – JWK Publishing 2013

Scorch

Previously Unpublished

The Teppenyaki of Truth

Originally Published in 'Splatterpunk Saints' – JWK Publishing 2013

Before the Meat Time

Previously Unpublished

Hope Eternal

Previously Unpublished

The Last Patrol

Originally Published in 'The Sinister Horror Company Annual' – Sinister Horror Company 2018

Beyond the Book

Previously Unpublished

The Sinister Horror Company is an independent UK publisher of genre fiction. Their mission a simple one – to write, publish and launch innovative and exciting genre fiction by themselves and others.

For further information on the Sinister Horror Company visit:

SinisterHorrorCompany.com
Facebook.com/sinisterhorrorcompany
Twitter @SinisterHC

Lightning Source UK Ltd.
Milton Keynes UK
UKHW041000170919
349935UK00001B/6/P

9 781912 578146